TERMINUS

A thrilling police procedural set in Scotland

PETE BRASSETT

Paperback published by The Book Folks

London, 2017

ISBN 978-1-5499-0297-0

www.thebookfolks.com

TERMINUS is the fifth novel by Pete Brassett to feature detectives Munro and West. Look out for SHE, the first book, and AVARICE, ENMITY and DUPLICITY. It is followed by TALION, PERDITION, RANCOUR and PENITENT. All of these books can be enjoyed on their own, or as a series.

Chapter 1

For the indigenous dog-walkers and their wayward hounds, for the raft of ramblers with their knapsacks and maps, and for the curious tourists on the trail of their forebears, the climb to the top of the brae – though not taxing – was amply rewarded with an unfettered view of the rolling Southern Uplands. Weather permitting. For Callum Dalgetty, it was unseasonably dreich.

He braced his fragile frame against a gusting south-westerly, scowled at the cauldron of bubbling, grey clouds thundering overhead and flinched as the drizzle peppered his face. Mustering what little strength remained in his ageing body, he cleared his throat and, lest his words be carried out to sea unheard, raised his head and hollered with the contemptuous conviction of an exorcist intent on casting out the Antichrist.

'May the soul of Esme Sinclair and the souls of all the faithful departed, through the mercy of God, rest in peace.'

Teetering on the brink of exhaustion, he tossed a handful of cloying, sticky earth into the cavernous pit below, wiped his hands on the back of his cassock and looked wearily across at Alison Kennedy – the only mourner in attendance – as she struggled to gain control of her umbrella.

'That's us away, then,' he said, his tortured face ravaged by the wrinkles of a lifetime's burials. 'My rheumatism'll not be thanking me if I stay out here much longer.'

'Right you are, Father,' said Kennedy, taking his arm as they set off down the hill, 'will I see you back to the rectory?'

'Aye, that's kind of you, Alison. Will you stop a while or are you heading back to the home?'

'No, no. That's me done for the day, Father. I'd say a wee sit down and a cup of tea is just what we need.'

* * *

As a vibrant forty-nine-year-old whose idea of a good night out was a stuffed-crust pizza with a side order of buffalo wings washed down with copious amounts of pear cider at the Club de Mar, Alison Kennedy – blessed with the looks and the figure of somebody twenty years younger – enjoyed nothing more than flaunting her assets in a pair of skin-tight leggings and a clingy Lycra vest. However, as the manager of the Glencree care home – and fearful of hastening the demise of those residents with a cardio-vascular condition – she deemed an undeniably conservative two-piece suit more appropriate for work, even though it made her feel about as sexy as a holiday rep on a coach tour for the over sixties.

Avoiding the impressive but calorie-laden spread of cheese and pickle sandwiches, mini pork pies and assorted cupcakes so thoughtfully provided by the housekeeper, she sat in the gloomy surroundings of the lounge, mesmerised by the flickering flames of the roaring fire, and waited patiently for her host to return.

Dalgetty, casually dressed in a pair of black trousers, a black clerical shirt and a pale, grey cardigan which matched almost exactly the towel-dried mop atop his head, padded silently into the room and headed straight for the sideboard.

'Nice shoes, Father,' said Kennedy, tickled by his choice of footwear.

'You've Mrs Campbell to thank for that,' said Dalgetty, smirking as he glanced down at the chunky Adidas trainers. 'I think they make me look like a reprobate from the ghetto but I've got to hand it to her, they're the most comfortable things I've worn in years.'

'She looks after you well.'

'Aye, she does that. I mean, will you look at that food. It'll be a week before I get through that lot, and I'm not even keen on cheese.'

'Will I pour you a cup?'

'No, no,' said Dalgetty, as his bony fingers struggled with the cap on a bottle of Ballantine's, 'you go ahead. I'm in need of a tonic, myself. Will you take a drop?'

'I will, but what about the tea? Mrs Campbell will have your guts for garters when she finds it's not been touched.'

'She'll never know. There's a plant pot by the window that has quite a taste for it, now.'

Dalgetty heaved a sigh of relief as he eased himself gently into his favourite armchair and raised his glass.

'To Esme,' he said, knocking it back.

'Esme.'

'How was she? At the end, I mean.'

'As you'd expect, but at least she went peacefully, in her sleep.'

'It's bad enough not having any family to see you off, but to be in her state…'

'Och, she was none the wiser, Father,' said Kennedy, 'really, she was happy in her own little world.'

'Well, that's something, I suppose, but I'll tell you this – I'll not see out my days in that home of yours, especially if I can't even remember my own name.'

'Nonsense. You'd be well looked after.'

'No, no. If I go the way of Esme, you're to put a gun to my head, do you hear me?'

'I'll do no such thing. How on earth will I make it past the Pearly Gates with a murder on my hands? And a priest, at that.'

'Pearly Gates?' said Dalgetty, gesturing towards the bottle on the sideboard, 'fanciful stuff and nonsense.'

Kennedy fetched the Ballantine's and filled his glass with a generous shot.

'Stuff and nonsense?' she said, with a wry smile. 'Whatever do you mean?'

'I mean there's no such thing, lassie. You live. You die. End of story.'

'Are you losing your religion, Father?'

Dalgetty contemplated the question, slumped back in his chair and fixed her with a vacuous stare.

'How long have you known me, Alison?' he said, softly.

'Why, ever since you came to St. Cuthbert's. I was a wean so it must be forty-odd years at least.'

'Aye. That's what I thought. And in those forty-odd years have you ever known me to falter? To stray from the path? To ever let anyone down?'

'Of course not. You're as solid as a rock.'

'Well, that's where you're wrong. I've let myself down. This whole religion thing is just a charade.'

'I don't understand.'

'I don't have the faith, Alison. Not anymore. I don't believe a word of it. If it wasn't for the fact that they'll be putting me in a box in a year or two, I'd walk away now.'

'But you've always been so…'

'Dependable? Reliable? Trustworthy?'

'Aye, all of those,' said Kennedy. 'You're the best priest I've ever known. In fact, you're the only priest I've ever known.'

'That's not true.'

'Alright, it's not true. But the others are Presbyterians so they don't count. What's this all about, anyway? You're the last person I'd expect to fall off the religious wagon.'

Dalgetty swilled the whisky around his glass and hesitated before answering.

'Love,' he said.

'Come again?'

'I'm in love. Always have been.'

'With a woman?'

'Well, it's not a choirboy, if that's what you're thinking.'

'No, no,' said Kennedy, with a giggle, 'it's just that, don't take it the wrong way but… at your age?'

'I never realised there was a time limit,' said Dalgetty, smiling softly. 'Margaret Forsyth. We met just before I joined the seminary.'

'The seminary?' exclaimed Kennedy. 'But that must have been years ago. Are you telling me you've been in love with this Margaret Forsyth all this time?'

'I have.'

'That's heart-breaking, Father. Why on earth did you not marry her? Surely if you…'

'Because,' said Dalgetty, draining his glass, 'she didn't feel the same. To use some poetic licence, my love was *unrequited*.'

'I'm fair welling up here. What's brought this on all of a sudden? Why are you telling me this? Is it Esme?'

'No, no. It's Margaret. She passed away last week.'

'Och, I'm sorry. You must be devastated.'

'That's one word for it.'

'So, how did you find out? Did you keep in touch?'

'Aye. We kept in touch,' said Dalgetty. 'We saw each other three times a week, every week for the past forty years.'

'My God, that's incredible,' said Kennedy, 'but if you don't mind me asking, did she not marry herself?'

'No. She did not.'

'Do you not find that a wee bit odd?'

'I do. Sometimes I tell myself it's because she never found the right man. Most of the time I kid myself it's because she really did love me, but I was, shall we say, already spoken for.'

'You're killing me here, Father. That's the saddest thing I've ever heard.'

'It's not sad,' said Dalgetty. 'We still had each other. We were still the very best of friends, but the most painful thing of all was that I wasn't with her at the end.'

'So, it was quite sudden then?'

'Sudden and unexpected. She was as fit as a fiddle. Well, as fit as one can be at our age, apart from the odd...'

'Odd what, Father?' said Kennedy. 'Was there something troubling her?'

'She... she was like Esme. Och, she wasn't bonkers. It was early stages. Most of the time she was fine but she had her moments. She'd forget things now and then, but don't we all?'

'Aye, right enough. We do, indeed.'

'But she had home care, and myself, of course. Not that that's any consolation now. So you see, Alison, I've not only let myself down, and the church, but I've let her down, too. Ignore me. It's been one of those days. Have yourself a cupcake and pass the bottle.'

Kennedy dabbed the corners of her eyes with a handkerchief and stared at Dalgetty who, head hung low, looked as forlorn as a fawn who'd lost its mother to poachers.

'I could join you,' she said, 'at the service, I mean. That is, if you'd like me to come.'

'Aye. I'd like that,' said Dalgetty, 'although I've no idea when exactly it will be. They're conducting a post-mortem.'

'A post-mortem? Why's that, Father?'

'Lord knows. Probably because it took everyone by surprise. Especially her. Still, I have the pleasure of meeting with her solicitor tomorrow for the reading of the will. Not that I want or expect anything but in the absence of any family it appears I'm the nominated next of kin.'

'Well, if you need any help, don't be afraid to ask. I know how troubling it can be. Lucas will gladly lend a hand if there's any legal stuff you need to deal with.'

'I appreciate the offer,' said Dalgetty. 'And how is he? That man of yours, Lucas?'

'Och, he's grand. Same as ever, you know: kind, considerate, funny, and generous to a fault.'

'Still smitten, then?'

'Well, it's only been a few months, Father, but it feels right. Comfortable, you know?'

'Aye. Like a good pair of trainers,' said Dalgetty. 'He likes to help, at Glencree, I mean. Has he a special interest or is it just because he can't get enough of you?'

'Very funny. Lucas seems to have a knack of getting through to the residents but then again, he's had a lot of practice.'

'Is that right? How so?'

'His mother was in care, back in Holland. She died a while back, now.'

'Sorry, I didn't mean to…'

'No, no, it's alright,' said Kennedy. 'Anyway, that's why he likes to help, especially with the advice, it's his way of giving something back. I feel so sorry for them, you know? They're thrown into our care without a clue who they are and no-one to take charge of their personal affairs and there's so much to deal with.'

'I can imagine.'

'House, car, personal effects, banks accounts. That's why Lucas is such a godsend. If it wasn't for him, the government would get the lot.'

'At least that's one problem I'll not have to deal with, all this belongs to the church,' said Dalgetty with a sweep of the arm, 'including Mrs Campbell. I came into this

world with nothing and, I'm happy to say, I shall be
leaving exactly the same way.'

Chapter 2

If the queue of slow-moving traffic, creeping like a cavalcade of mobility scooters on the way to a funeral, wasn't enough to infuriate her, then being forcibly detained by the roadside at the behest of two overzealous police officers intent on booking her for speeding, dangerous driving and failing to comply with a stop sign, certainly was.

Infuriated by the unscheduled stop, Detective Sergeant West – determined to cut the ninety-minute journey from Ayr to the Dumfries and Galloway Royal Infirmary to under an hour – floored the Figaro like a bumper car at a fun fair, dodging red lights and roundabouts with the prowess of a rally driver on crack.

Heart pounding, she stormed through the entrance of the hospital and headed straight for the ICU where PC Ferguson, looking as vigilant as a sedated sloth, sat leafing lethargically through the sports pages of the Daily Record outside Munro's room.

'And you are?' she said, panting as she flashed her warrant card.

Ferguson, startled by the distraction, scrambled to his feet and tried somewhat irrationally to conceal the newspaper behind his back.

'PC Ferguson, miss,' he said, 'I was just… it's awful quiet here, not much to do.'

'Whatever. DI Munro?'

'In there.'

'Is he up?'

'I'm not really sure. The doctor's with him, just now. Shall I knock?'

'Don't bother…' said West, distracted by the sight of a familiar figure sauntering confidently along the corridor carrying two cups of coffee.

Duncan Reid, having swapped the clean-cut look of an eager young constable for something a little *edgier*, something a little *rough around the edges*, looked positively roguish in his worn-out jeans, black biker boots and weathered, leather jacket.

'Am I glad to see you, miss!' he said, with a boyish grin. 'DCI Elliot said you were coming down.'

'Duncan! This is a surprise, you look… different.'

'Thanks very much. I'm honing my *incognito* image.'

'Is that right?' said West, amused. 'So, that's why you've given up shaving and washing your hair?'

'Aye, something like that.'

'Sorry, I'm just joking, you look pretty… cool. Listen, it's good of you to come all the way from Gourock to see him, he'll be made up. On your day off, too.'

'Day off?'

'Well, you're not in uniform, so I assume…'

'This is my uniform, miss,' said Duncan, smiling proudly. 'I'm not a police constable anymore. I'm a *Detective* Constable. And this is my patch.'

'You're kidding me? Well, good for you, Duncan. I mean it.'

'Thanks very much. And that's not all, it seems I'm answerable to you for the foreseeable so we can find the bampot who did this, together.'

'I wouldn't have it any other way,' said West, nodding at the cups. 'Is one of those for me, by any chance? I'm parched.'

'It is now,' said Duncan. 'PC Ferguson, go grab yourself a coffee.'

'So, how is he?' said West as Ferguson ambled off with his tail between his legs.

'Aye, okay. He's as battered as a fish supper but he'll survive.'

Duncan stepped aside as the doctor – old enough to inspire confidence and round enough to inspire dieting – emerged from Munro's room.

'This isn't the stage door, you know,' he said with a scowl. 'If it's autographs you're after, you'll have to wait until he's released.'

'DS West. We work together.'

'Och, I do apologise,' said the doctor. 'McKay's the name. There's been so many folk coming and going, it's a wonder he gets any rest at all.'

'Really?' said West. 'What kind of folk?'

'Reporters mainly. Most of them local. Turn one away and another pops up to take his place. It's like whack-a-mole on the NHS. Why, there was even one chancer who thought he'd get past simply by wearing a white coat.'

'I'm not surprised. They've no morals, have they?'

'No, they have not. Still, it's a good job you've an officer here. Someone in uniform is usually deterrent enough.'

'How is he?' said West as she sipped her coffee. 'I know you've probably told everyone else but I've only just got here.'

'Well, he's a broken arm and a fractured collarbone, three broken ribs and a punctured lung but nothing that won't heal in time.'

'Poor bugger. Can I see him?'

'Och, I don't see why not,' said McKay, 'but try to keep it brief. I'll be back myself in about a half an hour. Oh, I should warn you, his face is like a bag of Liquorice Allsorts, it's that bruised. And he's on a ventilator. And a drip. And we've hooked him up to a heart monitor, too. Otherwise, he's jim-dandy.'

* * *

Apart from an incident involving the discovery of several dismembered body parts wrapped in plastic bags stashed behind a bath panel, which resulted in the immediate discharge of the contents of her stomach into a nearby wash basin, West was hardened enough to handle any situation with the emotional detachment necessary to remain objective when investigating a crime. Except, that is, for the sight of Munro lying flat on his back with a face as colourful as a Caribbean fruit bowl. Duncan, sensing her unease, placed a reassuring hand on her shoulder as she stared in shock at his motionless body.

'Oi, Jimbo,' she said. 'What're you playing at? It's lunchtime and you're still in bed.'

Munro chuckled at the sound of her voice and slowly opened his eyes.

'What's so funny?'

'It's not me, Charlie,' he said, as he pulled off the face mask and held it aloft. 'It's the nitrous oxide.'

'You haven't lost your sense of humour then.'

'No.'

'Pity.'

Munro winced as he hauled himself up the bed.

'Constable Reid!' he said. 'You're here too. Good to see you, laddie, but you needn't haven't bothered. I'm not worth taking time off for.'

'I've not taken time off, chief,' said Duncan. 'I'm here on official business.'

'Official business? Then why are you dressed like a dope dealer?'

'I made detective, chief. And I'll be helping DS West.'

'That's excellent news, laddie, I knew you could do it. But tell me, what exactly will you be helping her with?'

'This case, of course. The mysterious case of the disappearing motor car that knocked you for a six.'

'I see,' said Munro, slightly confused, 'you'll have to forgive me but the memory's a wee bit vague on that score.'

'Nae bother, chief. Just as soon as you're up for it, I've a few questions for you, then we can set about finding the nutter who did this.'

'I see. Well, there's no time like the present.'

'Are you serious?' said Duncan. 'The doctor said you've to get plenty of rest.'

'Och, doctors. What do they know? I'll order some tea. Might take a wee while, though, room service here leaves a lot to be desired.'

* * *

Munro huffed indignantly as the auxiliary nurse – an overtly plump, thirty-something who, despite her relatively young age, appeared to be using the tea trolley as a walking frame – plonked a tray on the side table, sighed despondently and shuffled wearily from the room. Duncan stepped forward, tipped three spoons of sugar into a cup and passed it to Munro.

'Here you go, chief,' he said, 'it's only right that you should have the biscuit, too.'

'*The* biscuit?' said Munro.

'Aye, there's a finger of shortbread here.'

'One finger of shortbread? Three cups of tea and one finger of shortbread?'

'Maybe they ran out.'

'Ran off the plate, more like,' said Munro. 'Judging by the size of that nurse I'd say there were three on that plate when the trolley left the kitchen. It's a good job I'm not in the room next door or there'd be none at all.'

'You can't say that!' said West, grinning. 'You'll get done for discrimination. Or something.'

'Wheesht! I can say what I like. I've had a wee bump to the head, remember?'

'Nothing wrong with you then, is there?'

'Nothing a decent brew and a fried egg sandwich wouldnae fix. How about you, Charlie? How are you keeping?'

'Yeah, all good, I suppose. Tons of paperwork, nothing exciting. Apart from that…'

'And you're heading up this case? Down here?'

'Apparently.'

Munro paused and sipped his tea.

'Do you still have the spare set of keys to my house?' he said.

'Oh, cripes, yeah. I forgot I had those. Do you want them back?' Charlie asked.

'No, no. I'm just thinking, you cannae spend three hours a day travelling back and forth from Ayr, you'll not get any work done. No, you go home, pack a wee bag and get yourself over to mine, do you hear?'

'Okay, great! Be just like the old days.'

'I hope not,' said Munro with a wink. 'Oh, and get some food in, I'll not be far behind.'

'What do you mean?' asked West, inquisitively. 'Not far behind?'

'Exactly that, lassie. I've told you before, a hospital is nothing more than a halfway house between the here and now, and the other side, and I've no intention of ending up in one of those refrigerators they keep in the basement.'

'Stop talking rubbish, you're here for your own good.'

'Utter tosh,' said Munro. 'As soon as I'm dressed, that's me away. I shall recuperate at home and that's all there is to it. Now, how are you, Duncan? Or should I say Detective Reid?'

'Top of the world, chief. I'm so glad you pushed me to go for it. I'm having a ball.'

'Well, you certainly look the part, I must say. How did you end up down here?'

'I had no choice,' said Duncan, 'I just went where I was told.'

'So you're stationed at The Mount?'

'Aye, your old stamping ground, chief.'

'And have you nabbed yourself any criminals?'

'Not just yet.'

'Well, let's see if we cannae get you started. I'll go first. So, having said my goodbyes to Charlie and young DC McCrae, I left the police office in Ayr and headed home. Now, if I'm not mistaken, I stopped off somewhere on the way. Is that right?'

'Aye, that's right, chief,' said Duncan. 'You stopped in Dalbeattie.'

Munro frowned and regarded West with a tilt of the head.

'Dalbeattie?' he said. 'Now, why on earth would I stop in Dalbeattie?'

'Don't ask me,' said West. 'I'm as much in the dark about this as you are.'

'You stopped to fetch some groceries,' said Duncan. 'We found a couple of carrier bags from the supermarket in the back of your car. And one from the butcher.'

'Aye, that's right. I did. So, what happened next?'

'Okay, according to several folk who witnessed the incident, they saw you drop a bag in the boot of your car and walk around to the driver's side, but before you had a chance to open the door, it came at you.'

'What did?'

'A white VW Golf. It took you and your wing mirror for a wee scoot down the street before tearing off.'

'And you're saying this was deliberate?'

'No doubt about it.'

'You're sure about that? I mean, there's no chance I could've stepped out without looking?'

'No, no. CCTV supports the witness statements. The Golf was parked on the opposite side of the street. It was there for twenty minutes or so, engine running, and as soon as you returned to your car, the driver floored it. Came at you like a Scud.'

'I see.'

'Sounds to me like whoever was driving was waiting for you,' said West.

'And how did they know I'd be in Dalbeattie?' said Munro. 'Unless it was Doris Stokes behind the wheel?'

'Only one explanation,' said West, 'you were followed. What else have you got on the car, Duncan?'

'White Golf GTI. Registration SF12 HLE. Damage, obviously, to the front nearside. We traced it on CCTV as far as we could but we ran out of cameras.'

'What about the driver? Can you get anything off the footage? Anything we could enhance?'

'No chance, miss. Tinted windscreen.'

'So, it's disappeared into thin air?'

'Temporarily, I'm afraid so,' said Duncan, 'but we're still looking. It was registered as SORN a couple of years back so it's not been used for a while.'

'That's not true,' said Munro. 'No car's going to start after six months off the road let alone a couple of years. That car's been used, take my word for it. What about the registration, is it legit?'

'Aye, chief. Tallies with the records at DVLA.'

'So, in the meantime, there's a chance it could've been running around with false plates,' said West. 'Okay, what about the address? Where was it registered as off road?'

'Prestwick, miss. Prestwick Cross, to be precise.'

'Hold on. Prestwick Cross? That's where Carducci's restaurant was. Oh, come on, Jimbo, please tell me you remember that.'

Munro, eyes wide open, stared unflinching at West and slowly raised his right hand.

'I do, lassie,' he said, in a flash of recognition. 'And if I'm not mistaken, that MacAllister woman was living in the flat above the restaurant. Duncan, who's down as the official keeper of the vehicle?'

'Fella by the name of Gundersen, chief. Lars Gundersen.'

Duncan, perturbed by the ensuing silence and the apparent face-off between West and Munro, hesitated before daring to ask the question.

'Have I hit a nerve?' he said. 'Does that name mean something to you?'

'More than you think,' said West, reaching for the door. 'Come on, I'll fill you in. Jimbo, stay put and get some rest. I'll be back in twenty.'

* * *

Although he'd experienced first-hand the awesome power of the souped-up saloons and high-powered hatchbacks at his disposal in the car pool – more often than not under the pretext of chasing down a suspect spotted several miles out of town – Duncan was not, in any way, fanatical about motoring. As long as it went forward quickly, and stopped even quicker, he was happy. The Figaro, he imagined, could probably do neither.

'Nice wheels, miss,' he said, grinning as he sat in the passenger seat, his knees almost up to his chest. 'Could you not have got something a wee bit… bigger?'

'Size isn't everything,' said West, grinning. 'But I'm sure you've heard that before.'

'Ouch! Below the belt, but well deserved. Is there any welly in it?'

'Nothing to make your heart race, but it gets me from A to B. Eventually.'

'You should bring it down the station, miss, let the lads give it a tune-up. You'd be surprised what they can do under the bonnet.'

'I'm sure.'

'That's me told,' said Duncan, jokingly. 'So, come on then, what's all this about Gundersen and Carducci?'

'Okay,' said West, taking a deep breath, 'aside from his restaurants, Carducci was also a dealer, meth mainly, and Lars Gundersen was his supplier. They met in Oslo.'

'So, Gundersen's Norwegian?'

'Yup. And get this, Gundersen disappeared a couple of years back which was when, coincidentally, Carducci started importing the crap himself.'

'You mean he cut Gundersen out of the loop?'

'Exactly. And surprise, surprise, he's not been seen since.'

'Okay. What else?'

'Carducci was having it away with a lady called Clare MacAllister. She's the manager of his restaurant in Prestwick, the one who lives in the flat above.'

'And that's where the Golf was registered as SORN. So, is there a link between Gundersen and this MacAllister lady?'

'No idea,' said West, 'but we can't rule it out. Anyway, we were about to nick Carducci, not just for the drugs but for money laundering and half a dozen other offences too, but he was murdered before we could arrest him.'

'Murdered? And you think it was Gundersen who killed him?' said Duncan.

'No. It was his best friend's wife, Heather Buchanan.'

'I'm getting confused.'

'Not only that, Buchanan's husband was having an affair with Carducci's wife…'

'My head hurts.'

'…and, to cut a long story short, Heather Buchanan's banged up for murder and both MacAllister and Mrs Carducci are doing time for various offences – aiding and abetting, accessory after the fact, etcetera, etcetera, etcetera.'

Duncan sighed and scratched the back of his head.

'So, what do you reckon?' he said, perplexed, 'Do you think this Gundersen fella's back on the scene?'

'I really don't know, Duncan,' said West, pensively. 'It's possible, I suppose. I mean, what with the car and the hit on Jimbo.'

'That's assuming it was him driving.'

'Well, I can't think of anyone else, and if it was him, he's obviously got a grudge for some reason.'

'Against the chief?'

'Maybe all of us.'

'Why?'

'God knows,' said West, 'but you don't take a car out of retirement and use it as an offensive weapon for nothing. What gets me is, we couldn't trace hide nor hair of him during the investigation and the Norwegian authorities gave up looking for him yonks ago, so if it is him, the question is why? Where's he been all this time? And if it's not him, then who the hell is it?'

'Do you not have any easier questions we could start with?' said Duncan.

'I wish I didn't have any at all. Look, I need you to call the office in Ayr and ask for DC Dougal McCrae, he'll fill you in and send you over the relevant files.'

'Roger that, miss.'

'I'm going back inside to check on Jimbo, here's his address in Carsethorn. It's not far. Get up to speed on the case and I'll meet you there as soon as I've packed a bag.'

* * *

PC Ferguson, looking as though he'd spent his coffee break downing half a dozen double espressos followed by a gallon of Red Bull, was back outside Munro's room where he stood as stiff as a ramrod, his head twitching sporadically like a pigeon scouting for food, as he glanced repeatedly up and down the corridor on the lookout for anyone suspicious.

'Miss?' he said, nervously, as West raced towards him. 'I thought you were in there with the DI and DC Reid.'

'Well, you thought wrong, didn't you?' said West, glowering as she barged through the door. 'Oi, Jimbo,' she said, 'I've just…'

Her words tailed off as a sinking feeling, not dissimilar to that experienced when an unexpected letter from the tax office lands on the doormat, gripped her gut. Her eyes darted about the room, rapidly trying to make sense of the discarded blanket, the rumpled sheets, the line from the saline drip dangling in the air and, more alarmingly, the disturbing sight of a crumpled Doctor McKay lying slumped on the floor like a sack of potatoes, his eyes as bulging and as bloodshot as a bullfrog with an aneurysm.

'Where the hell is he?' she bellowed as she checked the body for a pulse, wincing at the bruising to the top of his neck.

Ferguson stepped warily into the room.

'I thought he was here, miss,' he said, 'with you and DC Reid. I came back and the door was closed so… bloody hell, what's happened to him?'

'Well, he's not a sodding narcoleptic, is he? Find a doctor, quick, and we need back up. Now!'

'Yes, miss.'

'I want officers on every entrance and exit. And get to reception,' said West as she frantically dialled Duncan's number, 'see if anyone saw him leave. Duncan, where are you?'

'Car park, miss. Just leaving…'

'Don't go anywhere! Get your arse in here, now!'

Chapter 3

If asked by friends or colleagues to name the one thing that first attracted her to Lucas, Alison Kennedy would invariably refrain from mentioning – beguiling as they were – his entrancingly pale, grey eyes, his towering frame or his athletic physique which, for somebody the wrong side of fifty, was impressively taut.

Instead, she'd recall a fund-raising event in the grounds of the Glencree care home and tell of how his lilting Dutch accent, which gently pitched and yawed like a rowing boat on a lake, played like a melody on her ears.

'*Lucas Rietveld,*' he'd said, smiling softly as he introduced himself. '*And if you are not married, then I should like to know why.*'

Having had her fill of men who considered a deep pan pizza to be the epitome of haute cuisine, and who thought a football shirt was acceptable attire for a romantic night out, Alison Kennedy had all but given up on the dating scene, choosing instead to enjoy life as a fully-fledged singleton until, that is, serendipity introduced her to the suave, sharp-suited Dutchman.

And for Lucas Rietveld – a compulsive workaholic burdened by the weight of his own success, whose diary was full but whose social engagements amounted to nothing more than some polite banter with the staff at the Royal India restaurant – meeting somebody who was not only strikingly attractive but smart enough to hold a conversation on anything from Rimbaud to The Rolling Stones, was like manna from heaven.

Four months on and as enamoured as ever, she could forgive him almost anything, including being late for dinner. She watched, doe-eyed, as he sat with his tie loosened and his sleeves rolled up, twirling spaghetti around his fork, taking care not to drip any of the carbonara sauce onto his pristine, white shirt.

'This is *lekker*,' he said, 'what would I do without you?'

'Order a take-away,' said Kennedy, as she topped up his glass. 'How was your day?'

'To be honest, a little tiring. I've been finalising a few details on Esme's estate.'

'That's funny. *Estate*. It makes it sound like she was minted. Is it complicated?'

'Thankfully no. She left a will...'

'All thanks to you.'

'...so actually it's very straightforward,' said Rietveld, stifling a yawn. 'I already have the confirmation from the court to act as executor so it's just a question of going through the motions, but you know how it is. It all takes time.'

'Thanks,' said Kennedy. 'For sorting it out. It's kind of you.'

'Nonsense. It's nothing. If you saw somebody lying in the street would you offer to help?'

'Aye! Of course I would! You know that.'

'Well, for me,' said Rietveld, 'this is no different, and besides, I make plenty of money from my other clients so I see no need to rob the dead or the dying.'

'You're one in a million, you know that?'

'One in 7.3 billion, to be precise,' said Rietveld, as he drained his glass. 'Oh, and before I forget, I've booked a flight home. I leave tomorrow afternoon. From Edinburgh.'

'Edinburgh?'

'Yes. That way I can fly to Eindhoven direct, which means I only have a short taxi ride at the other end. Are you sure you won't come with me? I can easily book another seat.'

'No, you're alright,' said Kennedy. 'Sorry, Lucas. I know it's the anniversary of your mum's... you know, but I'm just not in the mood for looking at another grave, not after today.'

'I understand. Perhaps we can go another time. We could make a holiday of it.'

'Aye, two weeks in a cemetery, that sounds like a real hoot.'

'No, I mean...'

'I know what you mean! Do you Dutch not have a sense of humour?'

'No. Not really. So, tell me, how was the funeral? Not too distressing, I hope.'

'No, no. I'm used to them,' said Kennedy. 'It's Father Dalgetty I feel sorry for. The poor man was soaked to the skin but, stoical as ever, he saw it through to the bitter end.'

'He should be careful at his age,' said Rietveld, 'if he gets a chill it could easily turn to something more serious.'

'More serious than a broken heart?'

'You've lost me.'

Kennedy paused and bit her bottom lip.

'No, I shouldn't,' she said. 'Forget it. It doesn't matter.'

'What doesn't?'

Kennedy set down her glass and looked Rietveld in the eye.

'Okay, listen,' she said, 'you're not to tell a soul about this, promise?'

'About what?'

'Do you promise?'

'I promise!' said Rietveld. 'So, what's the big secret?'

'Father Dalgetty. He's been in love with this lady since before he joined the church and get this, they've been seeing each other every week for the last forty years.'

'No! But should the church find out, he could be…'

'Not like that!' said Kennedy. 'It was purely platonic. Best friends.'

'I see.'

'Anyway, she died last week and he's beside himself with grief. He even feels guilty for not being with her at the end.'

'That's too bad.'

'Aye, it is. Came as quite a shock, apparently. Took everyone by surprise. I reckon it was probably a heart attack but he says they're doing a post-mortem. Just to be sure.'

'It can't be easy having to deal with that on his own,' said Rietveld, with a sympathetic shake of the head. 'I mean, as a priest I imagine there are very few people he can confide in. You must be a great comfort to him.'

'Och, I never thought of it like that,' said Kennedy. 'Makes me feel sort of privileged in a way. Incidentally, I said if he needed a hand with anything on the legal side, you'd be glad to help, I hope you don't mind.'

'Not at all,' said Rietveld. 'Would you like me to call him?'

'Not just now. Best wait until he's seen the solicitor about the will.'

'So, he has a solicitor already?'

'Not his solicitor, you numpty! Hers. His lady friend. Margaret Forsyth.'

Rietveld glanced furtively across the table and refilled his glass.

'Forsyth?' he said, with a frown. 'Why does that name sound so familiar?'

'Beats me. Och, you're probably thinking of Forsyth Street, up the way.'

'Forsyth Street! Of course. Either the wine is going to my head or I'm even more tired than I thought.'

'In that case,' said Kennedy, as she scooped up the dishes and piled them in the sink, 'what you need, is an early night.'

'No doubt about it, that's the best offer I've had all day.'

Chapter 4

Duncan, perturbed by the change in West's otherwise blasé demeanour, bombed down the corridor like a human pinball – bouncing off the walls as he side-stepped a gurney and a wheelchair travelling in the opposite direction – before skidding to a halt at the sight of her crouching on the floor outside Munro's room, her phone to her ear, her face full of despair.

'Goddammit!' she said, snarling as she threw her head back in frustration. 'Bloody voicemail!'

'What's up, miss?' said Duncan, catching his breath as he joined her at ground level. 'Are you okay?'

West hit redial for the umpteenth time and spoke without looking up.

'It's Jimbo,' she said. 'He's disappeared…'

'What? Och, that cannae be right. He'll not be far, I'm sure.'

'…he's not answering his phone. Something's happened to him.'

'Miss, I think you need to calm down a bit, he's probably…'

Duncan stopped talking as West looked up and flicked her head towards the open door.

'In there,' she said. 'Your mate, McKay.'

'What about him?' said Duncan, as he stood and peered inside the room. 'Oh. I see. Where's PC Ferguson?'

'Calling for back-up. Right, Duncan, CCTV. Quick as you can.'

'Roger that, miss. And you?'

'I should call the DCI and...'

West paused as her phone warbled with the sound of an incoming call and allowed herself a wry smile as the name "Munro" flashed up on the screen.

'About bloody time,' she said, relieved. 'Jimbo, where the bloody hell are you?'

'Hello, Charlotte.'

West turned to Duncan as the colour drained from her face.

'Who is this?' she said as the line went dead.

'Miss?'

'It wasn't him. Someone's... Duncan, I need you to ring the DCI for me. I have to make an urgent call.'

* * *

Wallowing in the tranquillity of the empty office with nothing for company but a pot-brewed cup of tea and a four-pack of chocolate éclairs, DC Dougal McCrae – keen to locate the elusive Lars Gundersen and thereby succeed where the Norwegian authorities had failed – made constructive use of his time by researching, courtesy of Angling Times, the benefits of a carbon fibre fishing rod over one hewn from traditional bamboo while he waited for West to return. The phone call, though not unexpected, caught him on the hop.

'Afternoon, miss!' he said, trying to swallow a mouthful of cream cake, 'how's tricks?'

'Not good, Dougal. Not good at all.'

'Oh, dear. Well, how's the DI? Is he...?'

'Listen, Dougal,' said West, impatiently, 'sorry, but I need you to listen.'

'I'm all ears. Fire away.'

'It's Munro. He's gone missing.'

'What?' said Dougal. 'Missing? Well, where's he…?'

'Listen, dammit! Someone's swiped his phone. I need you to put a trace on it and let me know the second it's used. I need to know where and when. Got that?'

'Got it. What's he using?'

'Dunno. iPhone, I think.'

'Brilliant,' said Dougal, as he logged in to iCloud, 'makes my job a whole lot easier. Hold on… it's offline. The last location was the hospital. We'll have to wait until it's turned on again.'

'Whatever. Have you spoken to Duncan? DC Reid?'

'Aye, nice fella. I've sent him everything on the case.'

'Thanks, Dougal,' said West, 'I appreciate it. Now look, I'm going to be stuck here for the next couple of days but I need to nip back to my place to collect a few things so I'll try and drop by later, okay?'

'Right you are. Oh, miss, before you go, this DC Reid, is he…? I mean, am I…?'

'Relax, Dougal. I need you and your brains behind your desk, okay?'

* * *

West rose to her feet as Duncan, normally a picture of cool, calm, efficiency, returned with a face like thunder.

'Who's rattled your cage?' she said.

'Everyone, miss. Funny, isn't it? A state of the art hospital like this and they still cannae find a cure for a lack of common sense.'

'Now it's you who needs to calm down. Come on, spit it out.'

Duncan smiled and took a deep breath.

'Okay,' he said, 'uniform's here and the DCI's on his way.'

'Well, that's good, isn't it?'

'Not with just six of them, it isn't.'

'Well, we can't worry about that now,' said West, 'maybe the DCI can muster up some support. What about the CCTV?'

'They're downloading the footage from the last of couple hours now, they'll send it to me as soon as they're done. I've left Ferguson concentrating on the camera at the end of the corridor, he knows who's allowed in and who isn't.'

'If you say so,' said West. 'Actually, you know what? Get them to send that footage straight to Dougal, this is right up his street. He can find a bloody needle without a haystack. We need to concentrate on finding Jimbo.'

'That's if he's not been kidnapped,' said Duncan.

'That's what I like about you, always looking on the bright side. Okay, then, let's say he has. Let's say he's been kidnapped and it's Gundersen who took him, and let's assume he's still driving that Golf.'

'Okay. Last registered at the same address as Carducci's restaurant and that MacAllister woman. I'll get them to check it out right away.'

'Good,' said West, as a constable arrived to take up duty outside the room, 'meantime, I'm going... that's it! Home!'

'Already?' said Duncan. 'I know you have to collect a few things, miss, but is it not a wee bit early to...'

'Not me. Munro! You know how stubborn the bugger can be. Bet you anything you like, the miserable sod's gone home.'

* * *

Duncan, his vision hampered by the relentless rain, held his breath as he focused on the tail-lights, desperate not to lose sight of the Figaro as it blasted along the narrow, coastal road until, without warning, it came to an abrupt halt on the grass verge opposite a row of terraced, whitewashed cottages.

'I've got to hand to you, miss,' he said, as he slipped into the passenger seat beside her, 'you certainly know how to drive.'

'I've got a degree in road rage, me,' said West. 'Besides, it's easy if you know where you're going.'

'Aye, right enough. So, this is Carsethorn, eh?'

'Yup. The original one-horse town. Only without the horse.'

Duncan peered past West and scrutinised the line of houses.

'Which one's his?' he said.

West glanced to her right and heaved a sigh.

'Unfortunately, Duncan,' she said, 'it's the only one without any lights on.'

Duncan sat back and ran his fingers through his lanky, sodden locks.

'I'm so sorry, miss. Really, I am. I mean, finding him here would've been ideal but I suppose…'

Duncan winced as a sharp elbow to the ribs cut him short.

'We're in luck,' said West, smiling as she pointed out the plumes of smoke billowing from the chimney into the dark, night sky. 'I don't care how ill he is, I'm going to chew his bloody ears off.'

* * *

Aside from the plaster cast, the arm sling, and a complexion as colourful as a peach and banana smoothie, Munro – seated at the dining table with a large, single malt and packet of painkillers – looked surprisingly well.

'There you are!' he said, as West and Duncan blundered into the room. 'I've been waiting ages, where on earth have you been?'

'You what?' said West, bewildered.

'Did you not have time to go to the shops?'

'Are you kidding me?'

'Dear, dear. We've no food and we're out of milk. Duncan, I'm afraid I shall have to ask you run a wee errand for me, before we all starve to death.'

West, repressing the urge to batter her mentor about the head with the bottle of Balvenie, stared at him in disbelief.

'You've got a nerve, you know that?'

'I beg your pardon?'

'Have you any idea what we've just been through?'

'Och, you're over-reacting, lassie. Did I, or did I not tell you, I was discharging myself from the hospital?'

'Yes, but…'

'Well then,' said Munro, 'what are you havering about? Now, fetch yourselves a couple of glasses and sit down.'

'You're unbelievable, you know that?'

'Very kind, but this is no time for compliments. I would've telephoned but I appear to have mislaid my phone. It must be on the side table in God's waiting room.'

'It isn't,' said West, tersely. 'It's been nicked.'

'Stolen? Someone's stolen my phone, from the ICU? Who on earth would do a thing like that?'

'Probably the same bloke who had a pop at that Doctor McKay.'

'McKay?'

'Aye, chief,' said Duncan, with a smirk. 'In your room. He nearly killed the fella. We reckon he was after you.'

'Well,' said Munro, taking a swig of whisky, 'it's good thing I left when I did. It's just like I've always said, hang about in a hospital too long and you'll not be leaving by the front door. So, what's the official line on that?'

'We're saying it was a one-off, no apparent reason for the attack, probably a disgruntled patient.'

'Well, there's a fair few of those about. I've a mind to complain about the catering myself.'

'Oh, I've had enough of this,' said West. 'Duncan, you stay here, call the DCI and let him know we've found him.'

'Where are you going?' said Munro.

'Home. I need to collect a few things.'

'No, no,' said Munro. 'It's too late for that, Charlie.'

'Relax. I'll be back in a couple of hours.'

'Couple of days, more like, in that wee pedal car of yours. Besides, it's not safe for you to be out and about alone.'

'I'm a grown woman, I can look after myself.'

'That's as maybe,' said Munro, wagging his finger, 'but you listen to me. If this bampot's got a bee in his bonnet over something I may have done, then there's every chance he'll be after you too. And you'll not be hard to spot in that vehicle of yours. No, no, park it in the garage and first thing tomorrow, you're to get yourself something a little more discreet from the pool. Do you hear?'

'He does have a point, miss,' said Duncan, 'if that nutter is on your back, then…'

'Okay, okay,' said West, defeated. 'You're right, I suppose. Duncan, car keys, please. I'll go get us some food.'

'Right you are, miss.'

'You're not cooking, are you?' said Munro.

'In your dreams.'

'Good. After all that slop they served up in the hospital, I think a fish supper's just what I need.'

'Is it, now?'

'Aye, it is. I'll take a large one, please.'

'Anything else?'

'No salt, no vinegar, and a wee pot of mushy peas. Thanking you.'

* * *

Duncan, having commandeered the corner of the table as a makeshift desk, and safe in the knowledge that he'd not be getting behind the wheel until the morning, set up his laptop and joined Munro in a generous dram which, he'd been advised, would not only alleviate the stress of finding a dead doctor in a hospital, but was also a more effective form of pain relief than anything available in tablet form.

'Nice wee place you have here, chief,' he said. 'Cosy.'

'Aye. It suits me.'

'Is it just yourself? Is your wife not around?'

Munro shot him a sideways glance and took a slug of whisky.

'She's passed on,' he said. 'A while back, now.'

'Sorry,' said Duncan, 'I didn't mean to pry, I just thought...'

'Och, dinnae fret,' said Munro. 'I cannae say I'm over it, and despite what you hear, time is not a great healer. But I cope well enough.'

'All the same, it can't be easy,' said Duncan. 'Was it... I mean, did she?'

'She did. Aye. It was a fire. Somebody torched the house and she was inside.'

'Oh, Christ. Sorry. I mean, sorry for bringing it up, too.'

'You're alright, son.'

'Did you catch the fella who did it?'

'I did. Aye.'

'Well, knowing you, chief, I'm sure he went down for a long time.'

'As long as you can get, laddie. As long as you can get.'

Duncan, relieved at the sound of the door, knocked back his whisky as West returned.

'Oh, that's right,' she said, backing through the door, laden with groceries, a six-pack of beer and three fish suppers, 'you two put your feet up, don't worry about me.'

'I thought you were going to the chippy,' said Munro, 'not feeding the five thousand.'

'Four thousand, nine hundred and ninety-nine, if you don't zip it.'

* * *

Despite the fact that he could only eat one-handed, Munro – having feasted on nothing more than two slices of toast and a single finger of shortbread throughout the entire day – had managed to successfully devour most of his supper by the time West returned from the kitchen brandishing a bottle opener.

'Don't wait for me,' she said, as she glugged her beer, 'it'll only go cold.'

'You're too kind,' said Munro, stabbing his fork in the direction of her plate. 'Are you not eating that?'

'Give me strength,' said West, cursing as she answered her phone. 'Hi Dougal, what's up?'

'Miss. I've some news for you.'

'Don't tell me you're still at work?'

'Where else would I be?'

'Have you not heard of Tinder?'

'Very funny,' said Dougal. 'Is DC Reid with you? Does he have his computer handy?'

'Yup. We're all here. What've you got?'

'I've sent some stuff you need to look at.'

'Hold on, I'll put you on speaker,' said West, as she gestured to Duncan to open his laptop, 'okay, all yours.'

'Right,' said Dougal, 'I've edited down three files from the CCTV. Open the first, fast forward to 16:22 and play.'

'Okay,' said West, as they gathered round the screen, 'we're off.'

'Good. Now, see there? That's you and, I assume, DC Reid leaving the DI's room. Right, forward again to 16:28 and we see a doctor entering the room.'

'That's McKay,' said West.

'Okay, now look, right behind him, someone else and he's in a hurry.'

'Another doctor.'

'Stop the film,' said Dougal. 'Look at him. What do you see?'

'Well,' said West, frowning as she scrutinised the figure, 'he's what? About six-foot-tall, reddish-blonde hair and a beard. And he's wearing glasses.'

Munro sat back, chuckling as he shook his head.

'What's up with you?' said West.

'Good grief, lassie, can you not see? The man's a Viking.'

'Gundersen?'

'Who else?'

'Which is why,' said Dougal, 'he's not wearing any ID. And he's dressed like a lab technician. The only time you'll see a doctor wearing a coat like that is on American TV.'

'Bugger me,' said West. 'McKay said someone had tried that before. Can we get that image circulated, please, Dougal, we need everyone…'

'Already done, miss. Okay, on we go. 16:29. Wait for it, and… here's the blond fella again, leaving the room less than two minutes later. Fast forward again and you'll see a uniformed constable arrive and take up position outside the room.'

'That's PC Ferguson,' said Duncan. 'Thanks Dougal, at least now we know what Gundersen looks like.'

'Nae bother. Okay, play the second clip. This is taken from the camera outside the hospital pointing towards A & E. It's very brief. There he is, only now he's wearing shades. On he goes, through the car park and under the camera towards the street. Now, play the third clip, this is the same location but the camera's pointing in the opposite direction. There he is, he crosses the road, down the side street, and gone.'

'Bloody hell!' said West. 'Is that it? Have we lost him?'

'No, no,' said Dougal, 'keep watching and stop when you see…'

'A white Golf!' said West, excitedly. 'And it's a four door, same as the one we're looking for.'

'There you go.'

'Och, come on!' said Duncan, 'Dougal, I'm not being funny man, but that car has not even got the right registration, and there's no damage to the nearside, and it looks like there's a woman driving. For Christ's sake, I thought you were better than…'

'Hold your horses, DC Reid,' said Dougal, uncharacteristically raising his voice, 'if I were you, I'd reserve judgement until you're in possession of all the facts. Now, if you don't mind. Zoom in.'

'Oh aye,' said Duncan, 'that's made a big difference, that has.'

'The nearside wing mirror, it's held on with gaffer tape…'

'That means absolutely nothing.'

'…and the woman driving keeps looking to her left, and she's talking…'

'Och, Bluetooth, you numpty.'

'…she's talking to somebody in the back of the car. And there's something else. Shall I tell him, miss, or will you?'

'I'll let you do the honours,' said West, smiling.

'That woman. Her name is Clare MacAllister.'

'MacAllister?' said Munro. 'When did she get out?'

'She never went away, sir,' said Dougal. 'Suspended sentence.'

West glanced at Duncan and raised her eyebrows.

'I think Duncan's got something to say to you, Dougal.'

Duncan puffed out his cheeks and sighed.

'Aye, right enough,' he said, reluctantly. 'Apologies, pal. I was a wee bit hasty in…'

'Nae bother,' said Dougal, 'apology accepted. Okay, final thing – the number plates. They're false. The index number belongs to a '97 Vauxhall Vectra which apparently was scrapped after an RTA eighteen months ago. The registered keeper of the vehicle was…'

West swigged her beer, glanced at Munro and shrugged her shoulders.

'Well, come on, Dougal!' she said. 'Don't keep us in suspense, who was it?'

'...the owner of Kestrel Cars, miss.'

Duncan, dumbfounded, downed his drink, his eyes flitting between Munro and West.

'Och, come on, you two, you're doing it again,' he said, 'that staring-with-a-look-of-surprise thing. What is it this time?'

West sat down, flipped the cap on a second bottle of beer and stuffed a cold chip into her mouth.

'Angus Buchanan, remember?' she said. 'Remo Carducci's business partner? He was murdered in the back of a taxi owned by Kestrel cars. The perpetrator was one Tomek Dubrowski.'

'And that means, what?' said Duncan.

'Come on, Duncan,' said West. 'I thought you'd read up on the case. Dubrowski and Clare MacAllister were an item, in the broadest sense of the word.'

'Oh, aye. Of course they were.'

'Bring her in, Dougal,' said Munro, as he filched a chip from West's plate, 'and whilst we're on the subject, Anita Carducci? What happened to her?'

'I'm not sure you're going to like this, sir,' said Dougal. 'Anita Carducci got eighteen months.'

'Eighteen months? Is that all?'

'It gets worse. She's out already.'

'By jiminy, I despair,' said Munro, as he refilled his glass. 'There was a time when if you got eighteen months, you served eighteen months, not a few weeks in a holiday home. The whole point of a custodial sentence used to be to scare the crap out of the villains so's they wouldnae want to go back. All this talk of rehabilitation and violating their human rights by denying them a television set and an en-suite is preposterous.'

'You're showing your age, Jimbo,' said West with a smile, 'we're all PC now.'

'Och, you can mock, Charlie, but I'll tell you this for nothing. The problem with the judicial system these days is it's broken. Aye, that's the word. Fundamentally. Irrefutably. Undeniably. Broken.'

Chapter 5

With his shoulders hunched and his head hung low, Father Dalgetty – as bent as a shepherd's crook – sat perfectly still, closed his eyes and, against his better judgement, muttered a prayer as the morning sun cut through the dusty air, bathing him in a biblical, sombre light worthy of a Caravaggio. His face, as leathery and as wrinkled as an elephant's hide, broke into a gentle smile as Kennedy quietly entered the room.

'Mrs Campbell said to come through, Father. I hope that's alright.'

'Of course, it is Alison, it's good of you to come. You'll not mind if I don't get up, I'm feeling a wee bit stiff this morning.'

'You stay right where you are,' said Kennedy. 'I see you've some tea on the go, will I pour you a cup?'

'Not for me, but you help yourself. Will I get Mrs Campbell to fetch you some breakfast? An egg, perhaps. Or some toast?'

'No, you're alright. I've not long eaten, myself. Lucas is away to Holland later so I made sure he had something decent before he left.'

'Off on business, is he?' said Dalgetty. 'I don't know how he finds the time.'

'No, it's not business, Father. It's the anniversary of his mother's death. He's away to lay some flowers and check on the house, that kind of thing.'

Dalgetty groaned as he straightened up and eased himself back in his chair.

'I'm impressed,' he said, 'you've got yourself a fine man there, Alison.'

'Och, don't be daft, he's only going to visit a grave.'

'You mark my words, it speaks volumes. I think it's shameless, pitiful even, the way folk are forgotten as soon as they're six feet under. We're none of us irreplaceable and as soon as we're done, we're tossed aside like an empty can of beans.'

'Still suffering from a dose of melancholia then, are we?'

Dalgetty smiled.

'Perhaps I will have that tea, after all.'

Kennedy poured a cup, passed it to Dalgetty and took a seat on the sofa opposite.

'So,' she said, 'how are you feeling?'

'Mentally or physically?'

'Both.'

'Like a shire horse on its way to the knacker's yard.'

'Oh, come, come, Father,' said Kennedy, with a reassuring smile, 'you're stronger than that. Now then, tell me how you got on with Margaret's solicitor. I assume that's why you've asked me over?'

'Aye, it is,' said Dalgetty, 'but I shouldn't be burdening you with that, it's not right.'

'Tosh. Something's troubling you, so come on, out with it.'

Dalgetty, frowning with frustration, paused as he gathered his thoughts.

'Och, I feel such a fool, Alison. And an old fool at that.'

'Take your time, Father. There's no rush.'

'I went to the solicitor's office, Hamilton's on the High Street, but when I got there, they said they weren't expecting me. Well, I said they were and I gave them the letter to prove it.'

'And?'

'Och, they were nice enough. They politely pointed out that the letter didn't come from them but from another firm altogether. I didn't even think to look. Took the best part of a day getting there and back.'

'Oh, dear. Well, no harm done. Maybe she changed solicitors and forgot to tell you?'

'No, no,' said Dalgetty, 'she's been with them her entire life. She'd not change on a whim.'

'Well, maybe,' said Kennedy, hesitating as she searched for an explanation, 'maybe they merged with the other firm?'

'No, no, they'd have said, would they not?' said Dalgetty, as he hung his head and sighed.

'Aye. Right enough, they would. That's not it though, is it, Father? That's not what's upsetting you.'

Dalgetty, his eyes fraught with confusion, stared at Kennedy and slowly tapped the arm of the chair with the palm of his hand.

'Many years ago,' he said, quietly, 'we sat down together and drafted our wills. I could've fitted mine on the back of a postage stamp but Margaret's… Margaret's was a little more detailed. Aside from the house, she'd saved a wee pot of money and she had some figurines, too. Things she called "collectables". Well, like myself, she'd no family to speak of, so she insisted that everything she had should go to a good cause.'

'That's very charitable of her, Father,' said Kennedy. 'I wish I'd met her, she sounds lovely.'

'She was. Anyway, she decided that when the time came, the house was to be sold and the proceeds divided equally between the Blue Cross and the PDSA.'

'Aw, so she was an animal lover, too?'

'She preferred animals to people,' said Dalgetty, 'and I can't say I blame her.'

'So, what happened next? Did you witness each other's wills?'

'Aye. We did. And we placed them in matching envelopes, and signed and dated them on the back.'

'So?'

'So,' said Dalgetty, with a sigh, 'the envelope the solicitor produced was not the one we'd used. And it was blank. Naturally, I queried this but he insisted it was hers and right enough, when he opened it, there was a will with Margaret's signature on it, but...'

'But what, Father?' said Kennedy. 'Whatever is the matter?'

'The animals. They got nothing. Absolutely nothing at all. I just can't believe she'd do such a thing. It's simply not in her nature. And there's something else, too. The will was dated just one week before she passed away.'

Kennedy rose to her feet, poured Dalgetty a second cup of tea and laced it with two spoons of sugar.

'That doesn't sound right, does it, Father?' she said. 'Here, drink this, it'll help.'

'And then, to cap it all, I went all the way back to Hamilton's and they said if she'd made a new will, then that was that, there was nothing could be done about it.'

'Do you recall who witnessed the new will?'

'Och, there was a name but I couldn't read it, and the signature was nothing more than a scrawl.'

'And how about the solicitor? Do you remember his name?'

'No. He told me when he introduced himself but it's gone. See here, what I don't understand, Alison, is why she left everything to a foreign charity.'

'A foreign charity?'

'Aye. The house, the contents, the money. Everything. She left it all to some outfit called The Schemering Foundation.'

'Are you joking me? What is that? German?'

'I have no idea.'

Kennedy returned to her seat, leaned forward, and rested her chin on her hands.

'Father,' she said, 'listen to me. I know you're upset about this, understandably, but something's clearly not right. Have you spoken to anyone about it?'

'Who would I talk to, Alison? And what would I say?'

'Even so, if you're that concerned, I think… I think perhaps you should tell the police.'

'The police? Really?' said Dalgetty, surprised. 'You think it's that serious?'

'Maybe not, but there's only one way to find out, isn't there?'

'No, no, they're busy enough. They'll not want an old priest calling them up about a dead friend's will.'

'Listen, Father,' said Kennedy, 'if they don't find anything, the worst that could possibly happen is you'll feel disappointed. Surely that's better than carrying around the not-knowing for the rest of your days.'

'Aye. Maybe you're right.'

'Good. I'll ring them for you, if you like.'

'Would you?' said Dalgetty, visibly relieved. 'Och, Alison, I can't thank you enough, that's a weight off my mind, really it is.'

'Nae bother, Father. It's a pleasure to help. So, you say the charity was called The Schemering Foundation and that's all you know?'

'Correct.'

'Okay. And what about the solicitors?'

Dalgetty pointed towards the mantelpiece.

'Up there,' he said, 'behind the clock.'

Kennedy retrieved the letter and turned for the door.

'I should be going, Father,' she said, with a comforting smile, 'you take it easy and I'll let you know what happens.'

Chapter 6

Without the mass of tangled wires taped to his chest or the incessant beep of the heart monitor ringing in his ears – a sound which, fearful it would change to a prolonged, monotonous squeal thereby signalling his imminent demise, prevented him from sleeping – Munro, feeling relaxed and refreshed, rose from his bed, dressed as best he could and made his way downstairs where Duncan, looking slightly the worse for wear, sat bleary-eyed in front of his computer.

'Morning, chief,' he said wearily. 'Did you sleep okay?'

'Better than you, by the looks of it,' said Munro, as he joined him at the table.

'It's that sofa of yours. It's wee bit small for me.'

'Dear, dear, dear, that will never do. I'll have a word with the staff and get them to fetch you a new one.'

'Sorry. Shouldn't complain.'

'Nonsense, laddie,' said Munro, 'it's me who should be apologising to you. I clean forgot I've a camp bed out back, will that do you?'

'Aye, I think so.'

'Good, we'll fetch it later. Now, have you heard from Dougal? Any news on that MacAllister woman?'

'Well, he's not phoned and he's not emailed, so I assume she's still on the loose.'

'Hardly surprising,' said Munro, 'she's as slippery as an eel swimming in baby oil, that one. Right, down to more serious business; have you had yourself some breakfast?'

'Not just yet,' said Duncan. 'I was waiting for you.'

'The one-handed chef? Think again. Two eggs, please, soft-boiled, and two rounds of toast.'

'Really?'

'Okay, make it three. Now, where's Charlie? Not still in her pit, surely?'

'No, no, she's long gone, chief,' said Duncan, as he made his way to the kitchen. 'I had uniform pick her up early so's she can get a car from the pool. She's probably home by now.'

'Well, well, well,' said Munro, smugly, 'that girl's turned a corner, Duncan, you know that? Not so long ago her waking habits had more in common with Nosferatu than us mortals.'

'Nos for who?'

'Never mind.'

'So,' said Duncan, 'have we a plan, chief? After breakfast, I mean?'

'A plan?'

'Aye. I've never had to babysit a convalescent before, so… I'm not quite sure what to do. Scrabble, maybe? Or a game of Monopoly?'

'Are you joking me? Does this look like an old folks' home to you?'

'Well, no. I just…'

'Look outside, laddie. Tell me, what do you see?'

Duncan, hands in pockets, shuffled across the room and gazed through the window.

'Sky,' he said. 'And the sea.'

'A clear, blue sky,' said Munro. 'And a calm sea. And glorious sunshine. Perfect day for a drive, wouldn't you say?'

46

'A drive? Where to? No offence, chief, but you're meant to be resting. I'm not being held responsible if anything…'

'Suit yourself,' said Munro, 'but I'm not sitting round here all day.'

'Well, where will we go, then?'

'Kestrel Cars, of course,' said Munro, as he pointed towards the kitchen. 'Toast. It's burning.'

* * *

Much to her embarrassment, the dull, grey Toyota saloon – capable of outrunning most vehicles on the road despite its outward appearance – was not the kind of nondescript vehicle she'd hoped for but an ageing rust-bucket with dented bodywork, no hub-caps and a rock-hard suspension which threatened to shatter her spine every time she hit a speed bump.

Cursing under her breath as she realised she'd left the remote control for the car park in the glove compartment of the Figaro, West pulled up outside the pedestrian entrance to her apartment block, sprinted up the stairs to the second floor, and froze.

A look of consternation crossed her face as her mind flashed back to the stairwell which, normally bathed in light, was unusually dark, and then to the main door, her key in the lock, and the subtle, splintering on the white, wooden frame. She turned, slowly, through one hundred and eighty degrees, scouring the landing from floor to ceiling, her eyes narrowing as she focused on the security camera, its blinking LED – dormant. The cable, running to a hole in the ceiling – neatly sliced in two.

Heart racing and her tummy as tight as a tourniquet on a severed artery, she pulled the phone from the holster on her belt and called Dougal.

'Stay on the line,' she said, softly, 'and don't say a word.'

With a can of CS spray gripped firmly between her teeth she walked slowly, heel to toe, along the corridor, grimaced at the same scratch marks by the lock on her front door, and cocked her head as she listened for signs of movement. Taking a deep breath, she slipped the key gently into the lock and stepped silently inside.

'Dougal? You there?' she said, relieved to find that the flat was clear.

'Aye, miss, what's going on? It's all a wee bit weird, if you don't mind me…'

'I'm at home, someone's been here.'

'In your flat? You've been burgled?'

'No,' said West, sweating as she hastily threw some clothes into an overnight bag, 'they weren't after what I've got, they were after me. I'll be there in ten.'

* * *

Peeved by the fact that DCI Elliot had saddled him with the seemingly menial task of garnering information on a foreign-sounding charity, and irritated further by its absence from the Scottish charities register, Dougal – unable to concentrate on anything in particular – huffed indignantly as he sat moping at his desk, waiting for West to arrive.

'Miss!' he said, leaping to his feet as she lumbered through the door. 'You've had me worried, are you okay?'

'No, not really,' said West, as her rucksack hit the floor. 'To be honest, Dougal, I'm a bit freaked out.'

'I'm not surprised. Sit yourself down, I reckon what you need is a decent brew.'

'I'll do it. Are you busy?'

'Nothing that can't wait.'

'Okay, first of all, I need you to ring Duncan. Remind him to pick up a phone for Munro, as soon as possible, and tell him not to let him out of his sight, not even for a minute, got that?'

'On it.'

'Second, I need SOCOs at mine, and make sure they've got uniform with them, just in case.'

'Is there anything I can tell them?' said Dougal. 'I mean, like, anything they should look for?'

'No, I don't think so,' said West, as she tossed him the keys to her flat. 'They didn't go rummaging through the drawers, if that's what you mean. Like I said, the doors were jimmied and the security cameras disabled. Not something your run-of-the-mill burglar would bother with.'

'And everything else was secure? Windows? Door to the balcony?'

'Didn't hang around to check,' said West, as she sat down and sipped her tea. 'There's only one person I can think of who'd want to take a look around the flat, and it's not an estate agent.'

'Aye. Gundersen,' said Dougal. 'This is getting serious, miss. First Munro and now…'

'Best not dwell on it, eh? Otherwise we'll all end up paranoid. So, Clare MacAllister. Any joy?'

'I'm afraid not. We took the liberty of letting ourselves into her flat, she's definitely living there, there's fresh milk in the fridge, plenty of food, etcetera. Just not her.'

'For crying out loud, Dougal! This is a priority; don't you realise how serious this is?'

'Aye, of course, miss! We've got an eye on the place and everyone's looking for her, but there's only so much we can…'

'Sorry,' said West, as she held up her hands. 'I'm just a bit stressed, I suppose.'

'Understandably so. You look done in and it's not even nine o'clock. Have you eaten anything?'

'No.'

'Here. Bacon toastie, if you don't mind it cold.'

'Mind? Are you kidding? Hang on, though, this is your breakfast.'

'Was. I lost my appetite when you called.'

'Thanks, Dougal. And sorry. I didn't mean to…'

'Nae bother, miss. Enjoy.'

West wolfed down the sandwich, leaned back in her chair and, allowing herself to finally relax for a moment or two, heaved a sigh as Dougal presented her with a second mug of tea.

'So,' she said, 'what are you up to? Anything exciting?'

'Och, no,' said Dougal, 'nothing important, just something DCI Elliot dumped on me. Should be out of the way in a couple of hours.'

'Okay, so long as you don't get too distracted, I need you on this, okay? What is it, anyway?'

'Some priest over in Maybole, name of Dalgetty, he says his best friend died but the will she left is not the one she wrote. Apparently.'

'Intriguing. So, what do you reckon, fraud by deception?'

'No,' said Dougal, laughing. 'Are you joking me? Somebody writing fraudulent wills? In Maybole? No, no. I can't see it, myself.'

'How far have you got?'

'Well, I went to the solicitor's office this morning but there was no-one there.'

'Not everyone gets up at five am, Dougal.'

'Right enough. I'll try again later.'

'This Dalgetty bloke, though,' said West, 'he's obviously concerned otherwise he wouldn't have called us in.'

'Aye, but even so, do you not think it all sounds a bit far-fetched. Besides, it wasn't him who contacted us, it was a woman by the name of Alison Kennedy. Manager of the Glencree care home. They go back years, apparently.'

'Well, maybe you should be talking to her.'

'She's next on my list, miss.'

'Good,' said West, 'well, I've got enough on my plate, so I'll leave you to it. Keep me posted.'

Chapter 7

With bags under his eyes, an itchy beard, and, as a result of his impromptu overnight stay, no change of clothes, Duncan – whose image had regressed from street-wise dope dealer to that of a borderline vagrant – drew dozens of curious glances from suspicious passers-by as he loitered outside the taxi office on Smith Street, waiting for Munro to catch up.

'Look, chief,' he said, smirking as he pointed to the sign above the door, '*Kestrel Cars – We'll take you for a ride.*'

'At least they're honest,' said Munro, 'cannae fault them for that.'

* * *

The controller, a bespectacled, white-haired lady with a face as full as a harvest moon, peeked out from behind the sliding, glass window in the wood-panelled wall and gasped as she caught sight of Munro.

'Morning gents,' she said, nervously, 'are you sure it's a taxi you're wanting, and not an ambulance?'

'I may look like a Battenberg cake, madam,' said Munro with an affable smile, 'but I can assure you I'm perfectly well.'

'Can we have a word with the owner, please,' said Duncan as he flashed his warrant card, 'won't take long.'

The lady hesitated before disappearing from view.

'Jazz!' she called. 'You've company. It's the police.'

A clean-shaven, Indian man of average height and average build dressed in jeans and a polo shirt, with an unruly mop of hair, wandered into the foyer.

'Alright?' he said, as he proffered his hand. 'Jazz. What can I do you for?'

'DC Reid,' said Duncan, 'and this is DI Munro. Jazz? That's an unusual name.'

'It's easier to remember than Jasminder Banerjee.'

'Right enough. You're not from round here, are you?'

Jazz frowned and glanced at Munro.

'Is he for real?' he said, with a flick of the head.

'No, no,' said Duncan, apologetically, 'I didn't mean it like that, I meant…'

'Relax, you dafty. I'm joking you. Dundee. Born and bred.'

'I thought so. It's the accent. Mind if we ask you a couple of questions?'

'Ask away. Is this something to do with Tommy?'

'Tomek Dubrowski?' said Munro. 'Not directly, but aye, in a manner of speaking.'

'I thought that was all done and dusted. Is that bampot not behind bars?'

'He is,' said Munro, 'but see here, Jazz, we're trying to trace a particular vehicle and I thought you could maybe help us out. It's a Volkswagen Golf…'

'I can stop you there, Inspector,' said Jazz, raising his hand. 'All my cars are saloons. Hybrids. Even the owner-drivers. There's no way I could use a hatchback as a minicab.'

'Fair enough,' said Duncan, 'but the thing is, this Golf we're after, the registration belonged to one of your cars, one that was scrapped a while back.'

'The Vectra?' said Jazz, with an inquisitive frown.

'You remember?'

'I'll not forget. It was almost brand new.'

'What happened?'

'An off-duty dunderheid, too much alcohol and a lamp post,' said Jazz. 'Ever since then, anyone using one of my fleet has to return it at the end of their shift, I'll not let them take it home.'

'How many do you have?' said Duncan.

'Six. All in mint condition.'

'And where do you keep them?'

'We've a small yard down the back, there.'

'Could we take a look?' said Munro.

'Aye, no bother,' said Jazz, 'but why the interest in my yard?'

'Och, curiosity, that's all. Just curiosity.'

* * *

Jazz wrestled with the padlock on the black, timber gate, released the ground bolt and, walking backwards, heaved it open.

'After you gents,' he said, proudly, as he waved his arm and beckoned them inside.

Munro's eyes drifted along the row of neatly parked cars – all identical, all sporting a yellow wheel clamp, and all silver. Except for the one at the end. Duncan turned away as he reached for his radio and made a call.

Jazz, wide-eyed with astonishment, stared at Munro.

'I've never seen that car before,' he said as they walked briskly towards the Golf. 'I swear, Inspector, I have no idea…'

'I believe you, Jazz. Strange as it may seem, I believe you.'

'You do?'

'Aye. I do. But see here, if I find out later down the line that you're lying, then trust me, you'll not want to be on the receiving end. Do I make myself clear?'

Munro strolled around the car, peered through the windows and stopped to inspect the damage to the front nearside as Duncan sidled up beside him.

'On their way, chief,' he said, 'uniform and forensics.'

'Good lad,' said Munro, wincing at the broken wing mirror, 'Jazz, I suggest you call in your other drivers, none of these vehicles will be leaving here for the foreseeable, okay?'

'Nae bother. Anything else?'

'Aye. There is. That Vectra of yours, who knew it'd been scrapped?'

'Everyone, I guess,' said Jazz, shrugging his shoulders, 'let's face it, in a place like this, a new car getting written off soon becomes common knowledge.'

Munro ambled over to one of the fleet and, relieved to take the weight off his feet, perched himself on the edge on the bonnet.

'Tell me, Jazz,' he said, gazing at the ground, 'how often do you check this yard?'

'Personally? Once a week, maybe twice.'

'Is that all?'

'Aye. I just make sure it's clean and tidy, and then I give the cars a once over.'

'And the last time you looked?'

'Day before yesterday, when we opened up.'

'Your drivers,' said Duncan, 'would they not think it a wee bit odd if they came here and saw a strange car parked down the end? Would they not tell you?'

'No,' said Jazz, 'a few of the lads often leave their own cars here while they're working, so, no big deal, really.'

'And apart from yourself, it's just your drivers that have access?'

'Aye, that's right,' said Jazz. 'They collect the key from whoever's on the desk and return it as soon as they've got the car.'

'And none of them owns a Golf?'

'No idea.'

'Has anyone been late returning the key recently?' said Duncan. 'I mean, could someone have taken it and got a duplicate cut?'

'Impossible,' said Jazz with a knowing smile. 'They're security keys, you'll not find anyone to cut them around here, they have to be ordered. And they're not cheap, either.'

'How many do you have?'

'Three. One for me, one in the safe, and one on the desk.'

'And the controller has responsibility for the one on the desk?' said Munro.

'Correct.'

'And they wouldnae take it home with them?'

'No, no, it goes back in the safe once we're done for the day.'

Munro frowned, stood and stretched his legs, and walked slowly towards the Golf.

'You're not twenty-four hours, are you, Jazz?' he said, pensively.

'No, Inspector. Too much hassle and not enough trade. We open at seven, then it's midnight weekdays, and two am weekends. Is that relevant?'

'Oh, aye,' said Duncan, confidently butting in. 'You see, Jazz, that Golf was probably parked here when you were closed, so someone with access to the keys has to be involved. We'll need to speak to all of your staff, okay?'

'I'll get you a list,' said Jazz as he sprinted towards the office, 'two minutes.'

'So, chief,' said Duncan, 'what do you reckon? Am I right, or am I right?'

'Possibly,' said Munro with a sneer, 'but you're suffering from tunnel vision, laddie. Remember, there's more than one way to skin a cat, and at the moment you've not even familiarised yourself with the knife.'

'You've lost me.'

'Good grief, man! Think about it! A driver shows up for work as normal, collects the key, opens the gate. The Golf is here, waiting, and parks inside while the driver takes his Prius out.'

'Crap,' said Duncan. 'Sorry. Question is – who?'

'Someone who knows Gundersen, of course.'

'Here you go, gents,' said Jazz, barely out of breath as he handed over a sheet of A4. 'Names, addresses and phone numbers.'

'Thanking you,' said Munro. 'Commendably efficient.'

'Have you any cameras about the place?' said Duncan. 'I mean, with six new cars sitting there, you'd be daft not to, right?'

'Behind you,' said Jazz.

'Can we get the footage off that?'

'No.'

'Come again?'

'It's a dummy.'

'Great,' said Duncan. 'Nae bother, we'll see if there's any on the street on our way out.'

'One more thing before we attend to these officers,' said Munro, smiling as he acknowledged the patrol car pulling up outside the gate. 'How many controllers do you employ?'

'Four. That's Beth or Aletta by day. And Robbie or Clare by night.'

'Okay, and Beth is the lady we've just met?'

'Aye, that's her.'

'And Aletta…?'

'Is my wife. And Robbie is my brother-in-law.'

'And Clare?'

'Friend of a friend. Ex-friend. Tommy.'

'Dubrowski?' said Munro. 'Are you telling me it's Clare MacAllister?'

'Aye. She came pleading for a job when Carducci's went under,' said Jazz. 'What could I say?'

'When's she due back?'

'Next week, I think. Check with Beth. Holidays.'

'Hold on,' said Duncan, 'sorry, Jazz, there's something I'm not getting here. Why would Clare MacAllister drive all the way from Prestwick for just a few hours work in a taxi office?'

'Prestwick?' said Jazz. 'No-one in their right mind would drive all the way from Prestwick.'

'But that's where she lives.'

'Then we must be talking about a different Clare MacAllister, because the one I know lives in Kirkmichael. Straiton Road.'

Were it not for the bruising about his cheeks, both Jazz and Duncan would have seen Munro's face blanche.

'Duncan, call Charlie,' he said, heading for the car. 'Straiton Road. That's Anita Carducci's address.'

* * *

Flanked by his two computers – neither of which could be described as useful or productive in his search for information on The Schemering Foundation or locating Munro's missing mobile phone – Dougal, rapidly losing the will to live, toyed with the idea of an early lunch and a trip to Gamesport to browse some reels, lines, and lures before deciding, conscientiously, on a visit to the Glencree care home instead. His departure was delayed, however, by the unexpected ping from the mac to his left.

'Crap,' he said, as he snatched the phone from the cradle. 'Come on, pick up.'

'Dougal. What's up?'

'Miss! Pull over! It's Munro's phone. It's been switched on.'

West, driving like an Italian on the way to Monza after a satisfactory lunch, swerved to the kerb and slammed on the brakes with scant regard for anyone travelling behind her.

'Go on,' she said, yelling at the phone, 'what've you got?'

'It's west of the train station.'

'The train station? Why the hell would he be catching a train?'

'He's not!' said Dougal. 'It's to the west of it. Hold on, let me see what's there. Okay, Kyle Street, the shopping centre… got him! I know where he is, miss! Smith Street.'

'What?'

'Smith Street! That's where Kestrel Cars are based!'

'Kestrel… Bloody hell! How the hell do I get there?'

'Where are you now?'

'On the High Street.'

'Perfect. Keep going, bear left at the fork, that's Kyle Street, it'll take you right there. Shall I send support?'

'No, no, no! The last thing I want to do is scare him off.'

* * *

West, unfamiliar with the area and infuriated by the crawling queue of traffic, dumped the car on the pavement and dashed down the street, her eyes panning the buildings until she spotted the office next to the pub.

Jazz, thinking all his Christmases had come at once, grinned broadly as the perspiring brunette in a white tee shirt and tight, black jeans burst through the door.

'I'm looking a for a bloke,' said West, panting as she held up her card.

'It's your lucky day,' said Jazz. 'I'm one.'

'Tall, red hair, beard.'

'Sorry. Short, black hair, sophisticated. Best I can do. If you want your pals, they're down the back.'

'Eh?'

'Your friends,' said Jazz. 'They're going over that Golf like flies round…'

'Golf?'

'Aye. Have they not told you?'

'Who?'

'Your two pals. The ones that were here earlier…'

'What two…?'

'The scruffy lad and the old fella,' said Jazz, 'looked like he'd bumped in to a baseball bat.'

'Munro?' said West, perplexed. 'DI Munro and DC Reid?'

'Aye, that's them.'

'When did they leave?'

'Oh, ten, fifteen minutes ago.'

'Wait here,' said West, pulling the phone from her belt as she scurried to the yard.

'Duncan, where the hell are you?'

'On the way to Kirkmichael. Where are you?'

'Kestrel Cars. He's here!'

'Who's where, Charlie?' said Munro. 'You're not making any sense.'

'For Christ's sake, Jimbo! Gundersen! Your bloody phone went off. We've tracked it here.'

'Okay, you listen to me. If that's the case, you might be putting yourself in danger, you're not to hang around, do you hear? Take yourself off and meet us at Carducci's place. Now!'

'Carducci's? Why?'

'Because, lassie, that's where Clare MacAllister's staying, and she's working for Kestrel Cars.'

'I don't believe it,' said West as she terminated the call. 'I just don't…'

* * *

Reluctant to leave so soon, West quickly scoured the street for a six-footer with red hair before jogging back to the yard and joining the SOCOs examining the Golf.

'Anything?' she said, addressing an anonymous-looking figure in a Tyvek suit.

'As it happens, we've quite a bit,' said the figure, removing her face mask as she stood, 'but it all depends on what you're after.'

'Anything,' said West. 'Anything and everything.'

'Well, we've some decent prints off the wheel and the door handles. Two sets, I reckon, so far. And they've left some of their supper behind the driver's seat – a takeaway chicken from The Rooster Hut with a half empty bottle of Pepsi. Should be able to get something off that.'

'Brilliant. Is that it?'

'No, no, we've only just started, but we've also found some hairs on the back seat. Red hairs.'

'Thank you, God.'

'Funny thing is, they're on the floor as well.'

'Is that odd?'

'I'm not sure, but whoever it was must've been cowering down there. And moulting.'

'Okay, look, please do me one, huge favour,' said West, 'don't wait until you're finished, get the hair and the prints off for matching now. It's, like, that urgent. Please?'

'Aye, okay,' said the forensics officer, reaching into a large, brown paper sack, 'and before you go, we found this as well, wedged under the seat rail.'

West made no apologies as she caught sight of the distinctive saltire on the back of the iPhone and began cursing like a sailor.

Chapter 8

Dougal parked his scooter on the gravel driveway, removed his crash helmet and stood back to admire the Gothic-inspired sandstone building known as Glencree which, were it not for the gargantuan sign extolling the virtues of the establishment, could have been mistaken for the stately home of a twelfth century laird.

'It's beautiful, isn't it?' said Kennedy as she strolled over. 'DC McCrae, I presume?'

'Aye, that's me,' said Dougal, offering his hand, 'and yes, it is. How old is it?'

'Not as old as it looks. Turn of the century.'

'Really? Well, it's certainly easier on the eye than the rubbish they put up these days. Most of these new-builds are about as interesting as flat-pack furniture, I mean, they're so soulless. No sense of aesthetics.'

'A man after my own heart, Constable,' said Kennedy, with a wink. 'Pity you're not a few years older.'

Dougal, lacking the social, personal and emotional experience to come up with a witty, sharp, and endearing retort, bowed his head and blushed.

'Sorry,' said Kennedy, 'I shouldn't tease. Shall we go inside or would you rather walk?'

'Let's walk,' said Dougal, his cheeks hot enough to fry an egg on, 'it's far too nice to be stuck indoors. So, about this will. I understand it was you who contacted the police, is that right?'

'Aye, it was. I couldn't bear to see Father Dalgetty so upset, so I said I'd have a wee word on his behalf.'

'Okay, why don't you talk me through what's happened, just so's I can get clear.'

'Well,' said Kennedy, clasping her hands beneath her chin, 'as a young man, Callum, that's Father Dalgetty, was intent on joining the church, until he met Margaret Forsyth, that is. He fell head over heels in love. Unfortunately, she did not love him. Or at least, that's what he thought.'

'But she did? Love him, I mean?'

'Aye, she did, but by the time he found out, it was too late. Callum had already joined the seminary and married God instead.'

'Dear, dear,' said Dougal, 'that's terrible. So, what happened next? Obviously, that's not the end of it.'

'Not by a long chalk. A few years after he was ordained, he returned to Maybole as parish priest and he and Margaret saw each other every week for the next forty years.'

'Och, a happy ending after all.'

'Not quite. You see, Constable, when they realised the years were passing quicker than they cared for, they each drafted a will witnessed by the other, which they sealed in envelopes and deposited with Hamilton's, the solicitors.'

'Okay.'

'Well, a few days after Margaret passed away, Father Dalgetty received a letter instructing him to attend the office for the reading of the will, only, the letter wasn't from Hamilton's. And the will was not the one she wrote.'

'And he's sure about that?' said Dougal. 'One hundred percent, no-doubt-about-it, positively sure?'

'He's adamant. There was nothing of any relevance in the will at all, nothing pertaining to him, or Margaret's beloved animal charities, or any of her other friends. Everything she owned went to some charity, "shimmering" something or other.'

Dougal stopped by a bench, offered Kennedy a seat, and sat for a moment in quiet contemplation.

'How was she?' he said, finally. 'Health-wise, I mean? Did she have any ailments? Was she on any medication?'

'No. That's why Father Dalgetty thinks it's so odd,' said Kennedy. 'Och, she had the odd turn now and then, but no more than anyone else her age. She was as sharp as a pin, most of the time. For Margaret to change her will so late in life and not even mention it to Father Dalgetty was completely out of character.'

'That's as maybe, Miss Kennedy, but a will is a personal thing, and there's no legal obligation for her to tell anyone about it.'

'No, no. I understand that, but there's something not quite right about this, Constable McCrae. Trust me, something's not right at all.'

Dougal leaned back and sighed as he scratched the back of his head.

'Look,' he said, apologetically, 'I can see you're both clearly concerned about this, and upset too, but…'

'If this is where you give me the brush-off, Constable, I can tell you right now, I'm not having it, okay? Look, Margaret Forsyth's new will was dated less than a week before she died. Now, does that not strike you as a wee bit odd?'

'Less than a week?' said Dougal. 'So, let me get this straight. What you're saying is – you and Father Dalgetty, you think she was, maybe, coerced into writing this new will?'

'Of course! I mean, why on earth would she go to a new firm of solicitors when she's been using Hamilton's for nearly sixty years? Ever since the day she bought her house?'

'Okay. Fair point.'

Kennedy glanced furtively at Dougal and cleared her throat.

'There's something else,' she said, taking a deep breath, 'and, I've not even mentioned this to Father Dalgetty. The firm of solicitors who dealt with her will…'

'Reed and Partner?'

'Aye. Well, one of the… I mean, one of the partners is my…'

'Is your what, Miss Kennedy? Your son? Husband? Boyfriend?'

Kennedy's shoulders sagged as she laughed with relief.

'Aye,' she said. 'He's my boyfriend. Sorry, it's just that word, *boyfriend*, at my age. It just seems so… inappropriate.'

'Och, nonsense,' said Dougal, 'so, your boyfriend, he's a solicitor, then?'

'He is. We've only been seeing each other a few months but…'

'Name?'

'Lucas Rietveld.'

'Okay, and you think he has something to do with this?'

'What? No! Goodness me, no!' said Kennedy. 'He's as straight as a die, good grief, the man's a saint. No, but I was wondering if perhaps… if perhaps his partner might be involved?'

'Well, it's certainly worth investigating,' said Dougal. 'I'll drop by on my way back. I just hope there's someone there this time.'

'You've been already?'

'Aye. First thing this morning.'

'You'll have more luck if you go now. If his partner's not there, then Emily will be.'

'And who's Emily? Some kind of legal secretary?'

'No, dogsbody, more like. She's a young lass, makes tea and answers the phone.'

'Okay,' said Dougal as he got to his feet. 'And your boyfriend?'

'Lucas? He's away just now. Back home in Holland. He'll be back this evening.'

'Right, you leave it with me, Miss Kennedy. I'll give you a wee call just as soon as I find anything out.'

* * *

The less than salubrious surroundings of Reed and Partner's office – located above an opticians on the first floor of an otherwise empty building on Killoch Place – took Dougal mildly by surprise. Unlike those depicted in the TV dramas of which he was so fond, there were no antique desks, no leather-backed chairs, no brass reading lamps, and no portraits of the firm's founders adorning the walls. Instead, the open-plan space was sparsely furnished in a style which would have been considered *en vogue* circa 1972.

He cast an eye over the beige, threadbare sofa, the two industrial-style tables, and the brown metal filing cabinet standing in the corner and concluded, somewhat cynically, that they'd probably been bought as a job lot from a second-hand furniture shop for less than fifty quid.

Emily Fisher, a petite, twenty-three-year-old with a face as innocent as grace, emerged from a small room at the rear of the office and smiled coyly.

'Hello,' she said softly. 'Can I help?'

Dougal, entranced by the vision in a floral-print dress with waves of dark-brown hair cascading down her back, fumbled for his warrant card.

'Aye, you can,' he said, stuttering. 'DC McCrae. Dougal McCrae.'

'DC? Are you a detective?'

'That's me.'

'How exciting, but if it's Mr Rietveld you're after, I'm afraid he's not due back until tomorrow.'

'Nae bother, you'll do just fine,' said Dougal, beaming. 'Sorry, what I meant was, it's actually his partner I've come to see. Mr Reed?'

'Och, there is no Mr Reed, Constable. Just Mr Rietveld.'

Dougal dropped the smile and frowned inquisitively.

'Is that so?' he said.

'Aye. I think the partner thing just makes the practice sound, I don't know, bigger, I suppose. More professional.'

'I see. Sorry, but then, who's this Reed fella?'

'That's Mr Rietveld. "Rietveld" means "reed field" in Dutch. A field of reeds.'

'Is that so?' said Dougal. 'Well, we live and learn. And how long have you worked here, miss…?'

'Fisher. Emily Fisher. Six months, or thereabouts.'

'And are you enjoying your work?'

'It's okay,' said Emily, raising her eyebrows, 'not exactly mind-bending, if you know what I mean. But I'm studying law, so it helps.'

'A wee insight into how it really works, eh?'

'Something like that.'

'Good. Well, see here, Miss Fisher…'

'Emily, please.'

'Okay, Emily. There's a document I need to take a look at, the thing is, I'm in an awful hurry and it's quite important, so I wonder, would you mind fetching it for me?'

'I'm not sure I'm allowed to do that, Constable. Client confidentiality, and all that.'

'I understand, but see, I only need a wee look, you can hang on to it.'

'I'm still not sure.'

'It's a will. The last will and testament of a Miss Margaret Forsyth.'

'Oh, that was dealt with recently,' said Emily. 'I remember because a priest came to see Mr Rietveld about it.'

'That's right. So, as the contents of the will are now public knowledge, perhaps you wouldn't mind…'

'Okay, I suppose that'll be alright, but you're not taking it with you?'

'No, no. You keep it here.'

'I'll fetch it for you now then. It's in Mr Rietveld's office.'

'Thanks. Oh, and Emily,' said Dougal, with a cheeky grin, 'before you disappear, have you handled any other wills recently?'

'A couple, aye.'

'Can I see any you have before Margaret Forsyth, as well, please?'

'I'll see what I can find. Hold on.'

* * *

Dougal, overcome by a primeval urge to appear more hunter than gatherer, loosened his collar and ruffled his hair as he wandered around the desks, baffled by the lack of paraphernalia usually associated with a sedentary occupation before contemplating, and then dismissing, a seat on the sofa for fear some of the beasties dwelling therein might migrate to his own clothes. He turned his attention, instead, to the impressive row of diplomas hanging on the wall above it – a QLTS practising certificate from the Council of the Law Society of Scotland, a bachelor's degree from Leiden University Faculty of Law, and a Master of Laws degree from Utrecht University. Unable to comprehend the wording on any of them, he took a photo of each just as Emily returned.

'Here you go,' she said, looking up from under her lashes, 'I could only find one other. Sorry.'

'No, no, that's great,' said Dougal as he flipped open the file, 'perfect in fact, although... you're not going to let me copy these, are you?'

'That would be quite unethical, Constable. Unless you did it behind my back,' said Emily, smiling as she turned around.

'Okay, that's me done,' said Dougal as he closed the files and handed them back. 'I'll take myself off and leave you in peace.'

'Peace is the last thing I need. There's too much of it.'

Dougal hesitated as he reached the door.

'Listen, Emily, I don't suppose you like fishing by any chance?'

'Fishing? No.'

'Pity.'

'But I do like motorbikes. And the outdoors. And reading.'

'Will I give you a call?'

'Aye. You do that.'

Chapter 9

At seventy-nine years old, Jack Kilbride – self-appointed guardian of Kirkmichael, unofficial authority on home security, and neighbour of the Carduccis – had carved out a successful career in retirement dispensing his encyclopaedic knowledge on the subject of absolutely everything to anyone who'd listen, particularly those tasked with repairing a lawnmower, renewing the guttering, or replacing the needle valve in a carburettor, thereby earning himself the reputation of a well-intentioned, but nonetheless interfering, old duffer.

Distracted by the stealth-like arrival of an unfamiliar vehicle, he postponed the unnecessary installation of a motion-activated security light by the front porch to snoop on the unmarked Audi A4 from a covert position behind the dry-stone wall, unaware that he, thanks to two well-positioned rear-view mirrors, was the subject of some curious counter-surveillance himself.

'He'll not make MI6, chief,' said Duncan with a wry smile.

'Folk his age should be indoors,' said Munro, 'dunking a bap into a bowl of soup. Or watching the racing on the TV.'

'Aye. Right enough. I think I'll have a wander, all the same.'

Kilbride, suffering from a sudden attack of the jitters, ducked behind the wall as Duncan stepped from the car, flexed his shoulders and ambled up the street towards him.

'Afternoon, sir,' said Duncan. 'We appear to be of some interest to you, can I help?'

'No, no,' said Kilbride, 'I'm just taking the air, thank you.'

'Okay, well, don't mind me. You just carry on.'

'Are you after something?'

'Nothing that concerns you, sir.'

'Oh, no?' said Kilbride, gasping at the sight of Munro. 'Well, I've got news for you, son, everything concerns me. Who are you, anyway? Are you on the run? Have you just escaped from prison? Is that it?'

'No, no,' said Munro, reassuringly. 'We're not on the run.'

'You're debt collectors, then? Bailiffs? You've come to rob some poor, retired pensioner of her television set?'

Munro smiled and shook his head.

'Police, then. That's it. You're the police.'

'You're obviously a very observant individual, Mr…?

'Kilbride. Jack Kilbride.'

'Perhaps you can help. We're looking for Mrs Carducci.'

'Best of luck, pal,' said Kilbride with a sneer. 'I've not seen her for days, and I've no wish to, either. Not after that terrible business with her husband being killed and all.'

'When was the last time you saw her?'

'About a week ago, I'd say. Maybe less. It was late. She came by in a taxi. I watched her go indoors, then I took myself off to bed.'

'And you've not seen her since?'

'I have not,' said Kilbride.

'Has anyone else been by?' said Duncan. 'Any visitors or callers, I mean?'

'Only the cleaner.'

'The cleaner?'

'Aye, which means Carducci's coming back, or she's planning to rent out that house of horrors to some gullible idiot with more money than sense. I mean, why else would she employ a cleaner?'

'That's a very good point, Mr Kilbride,' said Munro. 'Tell me, did you actually speak to the cleaner or is this just another one of your astute observations?'

'No, no, I spoke to her, alright. Nice lass, but a wee bit snooty for my liking.'

'When was that?'

'Yesterday morning,' said Kilbride. 'Just after ten o'clock. I was watering the roses when she came by.'

'Did you get her name?'

'I'm afraid not.'

'Do you remember what she looks like?'

'Five feet, six inches tall. Auburn hair, high heels, dark glasses. And she's a smoker.'

'Thanking you.'

'Hold on there, just a moment. You've not said, are you the police, or what?'

'I suggest you go indoors,' said Munro as West's Toyota came screaming down the lane, 'and make yourself some soup.'

* * *

Having established the whereabouts of the elusive Clare MacAllister, not to mention the discovery of the Volkswagen Golf, Munro – expecting to be greeted with a degree of enthusiasm for what some former colleagues would refer to as "a right result" – was taken aback as West let rip with both barrels.

'What the bloody hell are you playing at, Jimbo?' she said, shooting daggers and trying her best to keep her voice down. 'There's some nutter on the prowl who wants your guts for garters and you're driving around as if nothing's happened! You're supposed to be lying low and recuperating!'

Duncan turned to Munro and smirked.

'And what are you smiling at, Constable? You think this is funny? You're meant to be keeping an eye on him, keeping him out of danger, instead, you're ferrying him around like some sodding Dial-A-Ride service.'

'Have you eaten yet?' said Munro.

'What?'

'Did you miss lunch, Charlie?'

'Yes!'

'Och, well, that explains everything then.'

West, struggling to stifle a smile, took a deep breath and folded her arms as she attempted to reassert herself.

'Try the patience of a bloody saint, you would,' she said, shaking her head. 'Come on then, let's have it.'

'Well, miss,' said Duncan, sheepishly, 'we've found the Golf...'

'Yeah, yeah, been there, done that,' said West, glancing at Munro, 'that's where I found your phone. Have you got yourself a new one yet?'

'Not just yet.'

'Not just yet. No. Didn't think so. What else?'

'Clare MacAllister,' said Duncan. 'She's been working for Kestrel Cars ever since she lost the job at the restaurant. She gave Jazz, the owner, this address, which is probably why there's no-one at her place in Prestwick.'

'Okay,' said West, pensively, 'that means she and Carducci must be up to something.'

'And what makes you think that, Charlie?' said Munro.

'Why else would the mistress of Remo Carducci hook up with his wife? They're not united in grief, that's for sure.'

'Good. So, what do you think they're colluding about?'

'God knows. Money, probably. That's the only thing they have in common.'

'Is it?'

West gawped at Munro as he raised one corner of his mouth, encouraging her to think deeper.

'Gundersen!' she said.

'Hallelujah.'

'Remo Carducci and Angus Buchanan are both dead, suddenly Gundersen, ex-supplier, appears on the scene so, my guess is, he's trying to pick up where he left off and establish himself as the new dealer in town, and Carducci and MacAllister are in on it. Or they want a part of it. Or something like that, anyway.'

'Okay, so what will you do now?'

'Now? Well, keep an eye on this place until MacAllister and Carducci, show up, I suppose.'

'We've Mr Kilbride, for that,' said Duncan.

'Either way,' said Munro, reaching for his wallet, 'it means we've time for a wee quiz. Duncan. If I said to you "cow". What would you say?'

'Cow? I'm not sure, chief. Angus?'

'Good. And if said "chicken"?'

'Bantam.'

'And if I said "pig"?'

'Saddleback?'

'No. The correct answer is "streaky". Three rolls, please. Brown sauce. Café at the top of the street.'

* * *

West leaned against the car and smiled.

'Sorry,' she said, 'for mouthing off like that. It's just...'

'Och, water off a duck's back,' said Munro. 'It's nice to see you taking a stand at last. You know something, Charlie, you're not the lassie who wandered into my office all those months ago. You're a different person.'

'What do you mean?'

'Well, your best friend's not called Smirnoff anymore. And you've heeded my advice regarding the health hazards of sushi.'

'Yeah, and I feel better for it, too.'

'And you've got used to living in your own skin, again. You're to be commended, lassie. You've come a long way.'

'Thanks to you.'

'Utter tosh. So, you found my phone? Did you not bring it with you?'

'Sorry. It's with forensics. Cripes, that reminds me,' said West, 'I need to ring Dougal. Two ticks.'

* * *

Dougal, on the verge of a migraine meltdown as his head flitted from one screen to the other in an effort to determine the accuracy of Google Translate, welcomed the intrusion.

'Miss, am I glad to hear from you!' he said. 'I need you to look at something for me.'

'Me first,' said West. 'Guess where Munro's phone was.'

'Was it not at Kestrel Cars?'

'Yes and no.'

'Sorry, miss, but I'm about to perform a cranial lobotomy on myself with a bread knife, you'll have to elucidate.'

'It was in the Golf.'

'The Golf? The Golf was at Kestrel?'

'In one. So, listen. A heap of stuff's gone for analysis already, I need you to chase it for me. With any luck, the prints they've lifted will belong to Gundersen, so we need to…'

'We need to cross check with the Hordaland District Police in Norway. Nae bother. I'm on it.'

'Thanks. So, what's up? You need a hand with something?'

'A second opinion, really,' said Dougal. 'This case, the one with the priest and the will? It's looking very suspect indeed.'

'So, you think you're on to something?'

'Aye. I think I've found a connection. This charity, The Schemering Foundation, it's Dutch. It means "twilight" and was set up to help folk with dementia. Apparently. The funny thing is, the solicitor who drafted the will is a fella by the name of Lucas Rietveld, and he's Dutch, too.'

'And you reckon it's not just coincidence?'

'I'm not sure yet. I need to do some digging.'

'Okay, nice going, Dougal. So, how can I help?'

'If I send you a couple of photos, will you take a look?'

'Yeah, course. Send them now.'

'Sending. It's the certificates this lawyer has hanging on his wall,' said Dougal. 'They probably won't mean anything to you but it's not the content I'm concerned about, it's their authenticity.'

West opened the first photo and frowned.

'Sorry, Dougal,' she said, 'it's all double-Dutch to me.'

'Well done, miss. You're spot on. But it's not the language that's the problem. See, remember when you graduated and you got your diploma certificate, was there not something about it that said "quality"? I mean, the type of paper they used and the way it was printed?'

'Yeah, for sure. I think mine even had a red, waxy thing on it, if I remember correctly.'

'Aye, that's what I thought,' said Dougal. 'So, blow up the photo, big as you can. What do you think?'

'Blimey. Yeah, I'm with you on this, mate. It's got those streaks on it, like when you print it at home but the ink's running out.'

'That's just what I needed to hear, thanks.'

'Anything else?'

'No, that's it for now,' said Dougal, 'I'm waiting to hear back from the KLPD; I've asked if they've got anything on this Rietveld fella.'

'The who?'

'Dutch police, miss. I'll fill you in later.'

* * *

Munro, amused by the sight of a dishevelled Duncan tearing through a bacon roll as he swaggered towards them, gave West a nudge with his elbow.

'I've seen homeless folk better dressed than that,' he said, grinning, 'he'll be attracting flies if he doesnae do something about it soon.'

'Here you go,' said Duncan, as he handed out a bag each, 'one for you, and one for you.'

'Cheers, Duncan,' said West as she ripped through the roll, 'no offence but, as soon as we're done here, I need you to go home, shower, shave and change. There's a difference between being "undercover" and looking like you've just crawled out of a skip.'

'Gladly, miss. I must be honking, it's just that I've not had the chance. How long do you think we'll be here anyway?'

'No idea, but I think we ought to park up down the end, there, and wait in the car.'

'Okay,' said Munro as he headed up the garden path, 'you move the cars, I'm just going to have a wee peek round the back.'

'Oh, no you don't! You stay where I can see you,' said West as he disappeared from view, 'I'm not... I give up. I swear to God, that man's so stubborn, he must be part mule.'

'I like to see it as determination,' said Duncan.

'I'm surprised you can see anything through all that hair. Go and see what he's...'

West, fuming as the sound of breaking glass and a stifled holler cut short her lunch, cursed and dashed towards the rear of the house where a shamefaced Munro was standing by the back door.

'I lost my footing,' he said, 'I think I tripped on yon flowerpot.'

'You tripped?' said West, scowling. 'You tripped and your arm in the plaster cast just happened to go through the window?'

'Aye, and it's a good job it was the arm with the stookie or I could've done myself some serious damage.'

Munro reached inside the door and turned the key.

'Dinnae stand there gawping, lassie. Come on.'

* * *

The kitchen, dining room, hallway and lounge – minus Remo Carducci's cadaver pinned to the back of the armchair with an eight-inch carving knife protruding from his neck – were, on the whole, as they remembered them.

Munro, his one good arm behind his back, stood perfectly still, raised his head, and drew a breath.

'The air,' he said. 'It's stagnant. No-one's been here a while.'

'Not according to Mr Kilbride, chief,' said Duncan. 'According to him, the cleaner, MacAllister, she's been about the place.'

West, one eye on the street outside, watched as Munro took slow, measured steps around the lounge, stopping, stooping and scrutinising the sideboard, the stereo, the fireplace and the bookcase, before turning to face her, his expression devoid of emotion.

'What is it?' she said, recognising at once the look which had previously heralded the discovery of something particularly unsavoury.

'I'm not sure, Charlie,' he said, glancing up at the ceiling, 'but MacAllister wasnae here in her capacity as a cleaner. Everything's covered in dust.'

'Then what was she…?'

'Duncan, I need you to stay here, in case anyone comes. We're away upstairs for a wee nose around.'

* * *

Munro paused at the top of the stairs and, for a second time, inhaled deeply.

'Smell that?' he said, quietly.

'Can't smell anything,' said West, 'but then again, you're not normal, you've got the sensory perception of a bloodhound on heat.'

'Bleach,' said Munro, pointing to the door opposite. 'And, if I'm not mistaken, something akin to corned beef. You take that one, I'll take this.'

* * *

With its cast-iron bedstead, pine furniture and a commanding view of the wild meadow opposite, the main bedroom – decorated with a handful of vintage Italian advertising prints – was the epitome of rural charm. Munro, unable to reach ground level to check under the bed, limited his search to a cursory rummage through the wardrobe and the chest of drawers where the only items of clothing were those belonging to Remo Carducci.

'This one's clear,' said West, calling from the guest room. 'Bathroom.'

Munro, his brow furrowed with the weight of another conundrum, pondered why – in the absence of any ladies' wear, and when everything else had been tidied away – somebody would leave a solid gold necklace lying atop the dressing table.

West, looking as though she'd just swallowed an out-of-date oyster, poked her head round the door.

'I think I've found the mess MacAllister's been trying to clean up,' she said.

* * *

Despite her conviction for aiding and abetting, Anita Carducci had been guilty of nothing more than innocently executing the demands – albeit illegally – of the man she'd intended to elope with by transferring funds from his old business account in the UK to a personal one fraudulently held in the name of a deceased Norwegian national, abroad.

The vivacious fifty-two-year-old, blessed with an hourglass figure, chiselled cheekbones and plump lips, had – husband excluded – been the object of many a man's desires. However, lying face up in the tub with her eyes wide open, her frock caked in dried blood and her throat slit from ear to ear, she was not as attractive as she used to be.

Munro stared at the cadaver and solemnly shook his head.

'Open the window,' he said, wafting his hand in front of his face, 'it smells like a tin of Fray Bentos in here.'

'Poor cow,' said West, 'I mean, why? Who would want to do that to her? She's not exactly Ma Barker.'

'Right enough, Charlie. But somebody obviously had it in for her.'

'You're not kidding. But who?'

'I have my suspicions, and all will be revealed in due course, of that I'm sure. So. Observations?'

West made a cursory glance of the scene and leaned in towards the body.

'Well, she's as dry as a bone,' she said, 'and the plug's on the side, so she wasn't here for a relaxing soak. There's a trauma to the side of the head. She's got some nasty bruising around the temple.'

'Well, that didnae happen on the doorstep,' said Munro. 'Not with Big Brother living next door.'

'Okay. So it happened here. Indoors. Which means it must have been someone she knew. MacAllister?'

'Aye.'

'Right, moving on. Knife wound. It's not a clean cut, must have been some drag on the blade, probably dull or serated.'

'Good, well done,' said Munro. 'So. Conclusions?'

'Well,' said West, standing up, 'I'm thinking someone whacked her first, downstairs maybe, then dumped her here afterwards and that's when her throat was cut.'

Munro placed the back of his hand against Carducci's forehead then, using the plaster cast, attempted to lift her left arm.

'She's as cold as ice and as stiff as a surfboard,' he said, shaking his head. 'Rigor. She's been here at least twelve hours, although, judging by the scent of her perfume, I'd say it's probably closer to forty-eight.'

'Do we know if anyone's paid her visit?' said West. 'Friends, maybe?'

'Aye. That's Kilbride fella next door says he saw MacAllister leave around ten this morning.'

'Well, that fits. She could've done it, then. Last night?'

'No, no. Too soon. She wouldnae go off that quickly, but judging by the smears on the tiles and the tub, she's certainly had a go at cleaning up.'

Munro took a seat on the toilet, rested his chin on his good hand, and stared intently at Carducci.

'How tall do you think she is?' he said.

'Carducci?' said West. 'Hard to say. Five-five. Five-six, maybe.'

'Weight?'

'Dunno. Ten stone? Most of it up top.'

'And MacAllister?'

'Tall. Five-ten. And as skinny as a rake.'

'Exactly,' said Munro. 'Carducci wasnae dragged into the tub, she was placed there. And it's not possible for MacAllister to do that alone. No, no. This was a two-man job.'

'If that's the case,' said West, hesitating as she pondered the scenario, 'then it would have to have been

Gundersen, right? But the question remains, why would he want to kill Anita Carducci?'

'It's not difficult. Think about it, Charlie. Remo Carducci and Angus Buchanan were running the meth racket, right? Gundersen comes back and suddenly they're both away to meet their maker.'

'So,' said West, 'Anita was just a loose end?'

'Possibly. Or maybe she was after a slice of the pie and Gundersen was having none of it.'

'Bit extreme though, isn't it? To knock her off just for that?'

'Not for Gundersen, he specialises in extremes, Charlie. Okay, look, you need round the clock surveillance on MacAllister's flat in Prestwick, chances are she'll go back at some point.'

'Gotcha,' said West.

'What else?'

'Well, SOCOs, naturally. We need to find the blade that cut Carducci and whatever it was that walloped her on the head.'

'Good,' said Munro. 'You'd best inform DCI Elliot too. Tell him we're keeping a lid on this for the time being. Should any nosey neighbours or reporters come sniffing around, it was natural causes. Got that?'

'Got it,' said West, turning for the door, 'I'll sort the usual and circulate her details. What about an APW in case she tries to leg it?'

'Aye, why not. Keep an eye on the train stations, too. Oh, one more thing, there's a lady's necklace in the main bedroom. Bag it. It's not the kind of thing someone would leave lying around.'

Chapter 10

Based on the number of no-good, time-wasting, lazy low-lives she'd become embroiled with over the years – largely as a result of seeking out the physical rather than the cerebral – Alison Kennedy had, hitherto, considered herself to be an unreliable judge of character. Until, that is, she'd managed to snare, in Lucas Rietveld, somebody who made her content to the point of elation.

The fact that he was given to selfless bouts of philanthropy was an endearing trait but not one essential on her checklist of prospective suitors. The fact that he was wealthy – not that she'd seen any evidence of it – provided her with a subliminal sense of security despite her being independent and self-sufficient. It was the fact, over and above everything else, that she could trust him implicitly, which made him so attractive.

She poured herself a fourth glass of Merlot and sat toying with her phone as she constructed a brief but heartfelt message in her head, fearful of committing it to text lest she accidentally send it before it was complete, when her train of thought was interrupted by an unexpected knock at the door.

'Detective McCrae,' she said, swaying gently on her feet, 'what are you doing here?'

'Sorry, I should've called,' said Dougal, 'if it's not a good time…'

'No, no, come in. You're here now. Will you take a drink?'

'Not for me, thanks,' said Dougal, as his eyes darted around the room. 'I'll not keep you long. Are you alright, Miss Kennedy? You look a wee bit…'

'Och, nothing to worry about, I'll get over it. So, how can I help?'

'Well, I was hoping to have a chat with Mr Rietveld. You said he was due back this evening.'

'Aye, he was. The thing is, Constable McCrae, he's not coming.'

'He's been delayed?'

'No. He's not coming back. Ever.'

'Come again?'

'He called me from the airport,' said Kennedy. 'He said he's had some time to do some thinking and was of the opinion that we were going nowhere. So he's dumped me.'

'Sorry,' said Dougal. 'If I'd known… Perhaps I should leave you to it.'

'Don't be daft, you sit yourself down. How about a glass of water? Or I've some orange juice, if you'd prefer?'

'No, you're alright, Miss Kennedy,' said Dougal, niggled by Rietveld's reluctance to return. 'I don't suppose… I mean, did you by any chance mention anything about the will to Mr Rietveld?'

'No. I've kept that to myself.'

'Okay, good. And what time did you speak to him, today?'

'This afternoon,' said Kennedy. 'But I can't remember when, exactly.'

'Did he call you on your mobile?'

'Aye.'

'Would you check?'

'Clever man, Constable! Och, here you go. Twenty-seven minutes past four.'

'Emily Fisher,' said Dougal, muttering under his breath.

'What's that?'

'Och, nothing. Listen, did Mr Rietveld call you from Holland or after he'd landed?'

'I've no idea. Not that it matters, eh?'

'No, I suppose not. Look, I don't mean to dwell on the subject, Miss Kennedy, but when you say he's not coming back, is that just to here, or does he mean he's stopping in Holland?'

'Like I said, Constable, I've no idea,' said Kennedy as she knocked back the wine. 'He can rot in hell for all I care.'

'Aye, I'm sure. One more question and I'll get off the subject – would you happen to know which flight he was booked on?'

'I do,' said Kennedy, as she rifled through a pile of envelopes sitting on the table, scanning the back of each one. 'Here you go: Eindhoven to Edinburgh. Ryanair. Left at 15:10, landed 15:50.'

'Thanks.'

'So, tell me then, what have you come for? It's not a social call to talk about architecture, is it?'

'Not quite, no. Look, I cannae say too much as the investigation is on-going…'

'Fair enough.'

'… but I think you should know, Reed and Partner – there is no partner. It's just your… it's just Mr Rietveld.'

Kennedy hesitated and topped up her glass.

'No partner?' she said, frowning as she struggled to digest the information, 'so, what does that mean? He's been trading under false pretences or something?'

'No. It means…'

'Oh, Christ! It means if anyone had anything to do with scamming Margaret Forsyth, it was him! It was Lucas!'

'It's looking that way, aye.'

'The wee bastard!'

'I need to ask you something else,' said Dougal. 'It's nothing to do with Miss Forsyth so if you can't help, don't worry about it.'

'Go on.'

'Have you heard of a lady called Esme Sinclair?'

Kennedy froze and glared, open-mouthed, at Dougal.

'Esme?' she said, her voice quavering. 'Are you joking me? Oh, good God! Not her as well? He didn't…'

'You knew her then?'

'Aye! Of course I knew her! She was in my bloody care! Oh, Jesus, Lucas said he'd sorted everything out for her! He said he'd done everything in accordance with her wishes, that she… och, that poor woman, she'll be turning in her grave. If I ever get my hands on that conniving scumbag, I swear I'll…'

'Miss Kennedy, you're upset, I get that,' said Dougal, 'but you need to calm down. Look, I'm sorry about Esme, but I'm working on it, okay?'

'Okay,' said Kennedy, sighing with a deflated smile. 'I appreciate the effort, Constable. Really, I do.'

'Nae bother. Look, I really need to get going but before I do, would you happen to have a photograph of Mr Rietveld?'

'Aye, loads. You're welcome to them all.'

'Just one will do,' said Dougal. 'Head and shoulders. Can you email it to me?'

'Aye, I'll do it now.'

'Thanks. That's me away then. Is there anything I can do before I go?'

'No, you're alright,' said Kennedy, 'it's just a bit of a shock, that's all.'

'Understatement of the year.'

'I'm just glad I've found out now, and not later.'

'Positivity. That's good. Will you be alright?'

'Aye, Constable, I've another bottle in the kitchen. I'll be fine.'

* * *

Regretting the large pepperoni with double cheese, the bite-sized brownies and the half litre of Coke he'd swallowed in an effort to rid his mouth the taste, Dougal – pining for his toothbrush – scrolled through the list of alumni of Leiden University and glanced disdainfully at his phone as the name 'DS WEST' flashed up for the fourth time in ninety minutes.

'I'm scootering,' he said, under his breath, 'which means you'll just have to wait.'

The satisfied grin which crossed his face as he realised the results of his search matched exactly those from the University of Utrecht, soon evaporated as his phone rang for a fifth time.

'It appears,' he said, groaning through gritted teeth, 'I have no option but to pull over and take the call. Miss, are you okay?'

'Hi Dougal, been trying to reach you for ages!' said West. 'Where have you been?'

'Och, traffic, you know.'

'Traffic? On a scooter?'

'Aye, there was a… an accident. No, I mean roadworks! That's it. Roadworks.'

'Okay, let you off,' said West. 'I was wondering if the lab had been in touch?'

'No, not yet, but I'll chase them again if you like. How about you?'

'Oh, we're not long back ourselves. Hold on, I'm going to put you on speaker, Jimbo wants to say hi.'

'Alright, laddie?' said Munro, raising his tumbler of malt, 'how are you faring up there, on your own?'

'Aye, all good, sir. And yourself? Are you on the mend?'

'Oh aye, never better.'

'No sign of MacAllister?'

'Not yet. Not in person, anyway,' said Munro, 'but we do know she's been stopping at the Carducci house.'

'The Carducci house? That's odd. Why would MacAllister be staying there?'

'That's what we're trying to find out.'

'Have you not spoken with Anita Carducci?'

'We tried,' said Munro, 'but she wasnae in the mood for listening.'

'Och, that's no surprise. Playing deaf, was she?'

'No, no. She was playing dead.'

'Say again.'

'Dead, laddie. Deceased. Someone slit her throat and left her lying in the bathtub.'

'Are you joking me?'

'I'm not big on jokes, Dougal, as well you know.'

'And you think… MacAllister?'

'Aye. Plus one.'

'It's not fair, said Dougal, 'you lot have all the fun. And how's DC Reid shaping up? Still needing a go in a barrel of sheep dip?'

'Not anymore,' said West, grinning, 'he's smartened himself up and, guess what? He's right here.'

'Oh.'

'Alright?' said Duncan.

'Aye,' said Dougal. 'No offence.'

'None taken, pal. What are you up to? Watching the TV?'

'No, no, I'm just running through a few emails and…'

'Hold on,' said Munro, 'are you telling me you're still in the office? Good grief, man, you'll burn yourself out. What's so important that you cannae go home?'

'The Forsyth case, sir. I never knew folk could be so devious.'

'You're too trusting, that's your trouble,' said West, as she swigged her bottle of beer. 'Come on then, tell us all about it.'

'Okay, but you'll have to concentrate if you're to keep up. So, the firm that handled the will – Reed and Partner – well, there is no partner, it's just Mr Reed, only that's not his real name, as you know, it's Lucas Rietveld. He's Dutch. And the charity that got Forsyth's house, The Schemering Foundation, is Dutch too.'

'What a coincidence.'

'Aye, and no prizes for guessing who set up the charity which, incidentally, also got its hands on the estate belonging to one Esme Sinclair. She lived in Maybole and died not so long ago.'

'So,' said West, 'this Rietveld bloke's a bit crooked then?'

'More than a bit. See here, miss, he's not just some bent lawyer on the take. I've checked his qualifications from the certificates he's got hanging in his office and they're all fake.'

'So, he's not a solicitor, at all?'

'He never even went to law school,' said Dougal, 'and get this, I've had some help from a fella at the Dienst Nationale Recherche...'

'You what?'

'...The National Crime Squad in Eindhoven. Brigadier Mats Klassen. He says The Schemering Foundation has acquired seven properties in the last twelve months alone and they've since been sold. Now, here's the interesting bit: the charity's registered address is Koestraat 25, in Oirschot.'

'And that means what?' said West.

'It's not an office,' said Dougal. 'It's a house. A very large, very lovely house. It belonged to lady who died last year and, surprise, surprise, she bequeathed it to The Schemering Foundation.'

'He's some piece of work, this Rietveld chap,' said Munro. 'So, he's not just robbing folk over here, he's operating worldwide?'

'Maybe not the world, sir, but aye, the Netherlands definitely; but here's the beautiful part – the lady who owned the house was Lotte Rietveld.'

'Are you joking me?' said Duncan. 'You mean he fleeced his own mother?'

'No. That's just it. Lotte Rietveld didn't have any children.'

A palpable silence descended around the table as Duncan, West, and Munro eyed each other like a pot of poker players gambling their next hand.

'Have you got the evidence to back this up, laddie?' said Munro.

'Aye. Plenty. I reckon we're looking at fraud by false representation, theft, and obtaining property by deception. Klassen's sending me a copy of the foundation's financial records just as soon as he gets his hands on them.'

'And you think we have all the fun,' said West. 'Have you hauled him in?'

'I would if I could find him.'

'What do you mean?'

'According to his girlfriend,' said Dougal, 'he went to Holland to visit his mother's grave and was due back this afternoon. I've checked with the airline and he's down as a no-show, so I've requested a full passenger list for all the flights, just in case he switched to a later one.'

'And if he didn't?' said West. 'That means he could still be there.'

'Aye, right enough. That's why Klassen's heading to Oirschot as we speak and uniform are making a house call at the flat he rents here.'

'And that's it?' said Munro with a wry smile. 'That's all you've done today?'

'Very funny, sir. I'd love to stay and listen to some more of your one-liners but I'm away to my pit, just now.'

'I cannae blame you for that, laddie, but before you go, tell me, Dougal, are you familiar with the phrase "detective sergeant"?

'Och, what do you think? Why?'

'No reason, laddie. No reason at all.'

Chapter 11

Dougal, decked out in his favourite navy-blue blouson, charcoal chinos and trendy trainers, sat astride his scooter – helmet in one hand and an ice cream in the other – looking, to all intents and purposes, like a *donnaiolo* on the Spanish Steps, ogling the *belle ragazze* as they made their way to work, his temperature rising as he spotted one in particular walking directly towards him.

'That's a healthy breakfast,' said Emily, sarcastically, as she shielded her eyes from the morning sun.

'I'll have you know, this is near enough my lunch, Miss Fisher,' said Dougal with a flirty grin. 'Mind if have a wee word?'

'A word? And there's me thinking you'd come all this way to ask me out.'

'Aye, of course I did,' said Dougal, flustered. 'I just thought, two birds, one stone...'

* * *

Entranced by the sight of Emily perched on the table with her legs dangling a foot from the floor, Dougal – experiencing the kind of palpitations normally associated with the after-effects of a one hundred metre sprint –

unzipped his jacket, ran a finger around his collar and cleared his throat as he tried desperately to compose himself.

'Shall we do the boring bit first?' he said, nervously. 'Before we…'

'Anything you like, Constable,' said Emily. 'We can do anything you like.'

'Okay. Good. So, Emily, what I need to know is, did you happen to speak to Mr Rietveld yesterday? In particular, any time after I left?'

'Aye. As a matter of fact, I did.'

'Excellent. And did he call you or was it the other way round?'

'No, no. He called me.'

'And do you recall what time that was?'

'Some time after four, I think.'

'Bingo.'

'I'd rather go bowling.'

'No, no,' said Dougal, 'I meant… doesn't matter. Okay, this is important – did you tell him you'd had a visit from the police?'

'Aye, of course I did,' said Emily. 'Couldn't wait, highlight of my day. Week even. If not the year.'

'Okay,' said Dougal, embarrassed by the flattery. 'And after you'd told him, how did he react? Did he sound normal? Or bothered? Or…'

'Actually, now you mention it, he did sound a wee bit funny. Impatient. As though he'd been distracted by something.'

'And up until that point, you were expecting him back here?'

'I was.'

'But he suddenly changed his plans?'

'Well, I'm not sure how sudden it was,' said Emily, 'but aye, he said he had to visit some other clients and he'd be in touch.'

'Do you not think that was a wee bit vague of him? I mean, for someone of his standing, with his legal responsibilities, to not let you know when he's coming back?'

'Maybe. But who am I to question what he gets up to? As long as I get paid, I'm not that bothered.'

'Fair enough,' said Dougal. 'That room at the back, there. Is that his office?'

'Aye.'

'And do you ever have cause to go in there?'

'No, not really. This is my table, I do my studying here when I'm on my own.'

'Would you mind if I had a wee peek inside?'

'Feel free. If you tell me what you're after, then maybe I could help.'

'I wish I knew, Emily. I wish I knew.'

* * *

Dougal leant against the doorframe and let out a disappointed sigh as he cast an eye over the small, windowless office which – save for the desk, two chairs, and a stack of document storage boxes – was as empty as a pocket.

'Does he actually do any work in here?' he said, calling over his shoulder.

'Aye, sometimes,' said Emily. 'He brings his laptop and locks himself away.'

'Nothing else? No books, or notepads, or diary, or anything?'

'No.'

'What about the paperwork? You know, the official stuff his clients have to sign, or witness, or whatever it is they do?'

'That's all on his computer,' said Emily as she strolled into the office. 'He just prints it off whenever he needs it.'

Dougal, growing even more despondent, sat behind the desk, leaned back and tentatively pulled open the single drawer to reveal a rubber stamp bearing the company name, an ink pad, a stapler, a handful of paperclips and a USB memory stick.

'Have you used any of these?' he said as he snapped on a pair of gloves.

'No. I've never even looked in there.'

'Good,' said Dougal, sealing them in a plastic bag. 'I need to borrow them, okay?'

'Okay. So, is that it?'

'Aye, that's me away. I need to get these off, sharpish.'

'Are you not forgetting something?' said Emily.

'No, I don't think so.'

'Charming.'

'Oh, Christ! Sorry!' said Dougal, cringing behind the desk. 'My head's mince, I've just so much going on. So, what shall we do? Any ideas?'

'Pub!' said Emily. 'The Smoking Goat. I like it there.'

'Och, I'm not one for drinking, really.'

'Okay. Cinema?'

'We'll not speak for two hours.'

'Dinner then?'

'Aye, great!' said Dougal, relieved. 'What do you like?'

'Anything and everything. As long as it's vegetarian.'

'Oh dear.'

Emily playfully raised her eyes to the ceiling and smiled.

'Well, there's only one thing for it,' she said. 'You'll just have to come to mine. I'll cook some pasta. How about it?'

'Perfect. When did you have in mind?'

'Tonight, of course. Not point in beating about the bush, is there, Constable?'

* * *

Some members of society delight in dining in the stilted atmosphere of a triple-starred restaurant in the belief it might enhance their social status and view the challenge of translating *filet de cabillaud poêlè* into English, or endeavouring to unlock the mystery of a *pork secretos*, or attempting to determine the logic behind *deconstructed* banoffee pie, as nothing more than an exercise in mental agility. However, mused Duncan, little could match the simplistic majesty of a full, traditional breakfast.

Satisfied with his efforts as designated grill-chef, *Chez Munro*, he slurped his tea and let out a contented sigh as Munro – eagerly mopping up the remnants of a runny egg yolk with a slice of bread and butter – gazed yearningly at the rashers of bacon on West's untouched plate.

'Where is she?' he said impatiently.

'Not sure, chief,' said Duncan. 'Bathroom, maybe?'

'Well, if she's not here soon, she'll have to make do with toast and jam.'

'Someone talking about me?' said West as she breezed into the room.

'Aye. Your food's going cold. What's with the bag?'

'I'm heading back to mine,' said West, chomping through a sausage. 'I need to speak with that Jazz bloke again. Someone there knows who planted the Golf and I need to find out who.'

'Maybe, so,' said Duncan, 'but that's no reason to go home, is it?'

'You'll cope. Besides, I can't keep whizzing back and forth all the time, it's simply not practical.'

'It's not safe, Charlie, you know that,' said Munro. 'Someone's broken into your flat once already. Who's to say they'll not be back?'

'That's a risk I'll have to take. Anyway, the locks have been changed…'

'That'll not stop them,' said Duncan, cynically.

'Look, the only reason I'm down here, Duncan, is because Jimbo got walloped on your patch which frankly constitutes nothing more than an RTC. This case centres on Carducci and MacAllister and Gundersen which means I need to be in Ayr. End of.'

'That's me told.'

'Give me five minutes,' said Munro, as he cleared the plates.

'What? Why?' said West. 'Where are you going?'

'To pack a bag. I'm coming with you.'

'What about me?' said Duncan.

'You can follow,' said Munro. 'Take yourself off to Kilbride's place and trawl through his camera footage. See if he got a snap of MacAllister.'

Chapter 12

Anxious about the prospect of spending an entire evening alone with Emily in the intimate surroundings of her own home, Dougal – bowing to social etiquette – contemplated taking some wine as a gift for his host. However, without the necessary knowledge to make an educated choice, he dismissed the idea in favour of a bouquet of flowers before shelving the notion on the grounds that she may harbour a hitherto unknown pollen allergy. He opted for a ballotin of Belgian chocolates, instead.

He trudged up the stairs to the office, pushed open the door and paused, arrested by the sight of Munro and West casually sipping tea as though they'd never been away.

'Do vegetarians eat chocolate?' he said, tossing his coat to one side.

'Don't be daft,' said Munro, diffidently, 'too much protein. Their bodies cannae handle it.'

'Really?'

'He's pulling your leg,' said West, 'of course they do. Unless they've got a lactose intolerance.'

'Oh, God,' said Dougal, distraught. 'Lactose! I never thought of that. So, is this a flying visit or are you two planning on staying awhile?'

'We're staying.'

'I'm glad to hear it. It's been like working in solitary ever since you two left. Not one single soul has been through that door, not even a "*how's the investigation going*" from DCI Elliot.'

'You should take that as compliment, laddie,' said Munro. 'He obviously has faith in your ability. So, where have you been this morning?'

'Rietveld's office,' said Dougal, holding up the plastic bag. 'I need to get these off for dusting.'

'He's not back, then?'

'No. He's definitely avoiding the place, and uniform say his flat's empty, too. I'm going to have a mooch for myself just as soon as I've caught up with Brigadier Klassen. With any luck, I'm hoping they've found him hiding in the cellar or something. Where's DC Reid? Did he not come with you?'

'Aye, he certainly did,' said Munro, 'followed us like a lost puppy. He's with Carducci's neighbour.'

'Okay. So, what's your plan, miss?'

'First, I'm going to finish my tea,' said West, 'then, we're heading over to Kestrel Cars. Gonna listen to some jazz.'

* * *

West parked up, reclined the seat and closed her eyes against the blazing sun while Munro, trying to sate a troublesome itch beneath his cast, began to wilt like a water lily in a drought-ridden pond as the temperature rapidly rose.

'Charlie,' he said, as beads of perspiration gathered on his forehead, 'your phone.'

'What about it?'

'Answer it.'

'In a minute.'

'It might be important.'

'Then again,' said West, indifferently, 'it might not.'

Munro, experiencing something close to an epiphany, slowly turned to her and smiled.

'By jiminy!' he said, as if a weight had been lifted from his shoulders, 'you know something, lassie? You're absolutely right! I thought I might actually miss not having a mobile phone, but it's actually quite liberating. Aye, that's the word. Liberating.'

'That's nice.'

'In fact, I'm not sure I want a new one. Or the old one back.'

'Good for you.'

'I've the landline at home. And that's where I'll be once this case is closed, so, there's no need.'

'Nope. No need at all,' said West, sitting up with a start. 'Hold on, what if I need to get hold of you?'

'I told you,' said Munro, 'ring the landline. Or write a letter.'

'Have you seen the price of postage stamps?'

'Email, then.'

'Oh, no. You need a phone, Jimbo. I'll get you one of those ones that just makes calls and texts, with those great big buttons for the visually impaired.'

'You'll be joining that unfortunate group, if you're not careful, lassie. Now, for the love of God, will you answer your phone?'

'Duncan,' said West as she switched to speaker. 'What's up?'

'I'm with Mr Kilbride. He's kindly gathered together one hundred and twenty hours' worth of footage from four cameras about the house.'

'See you next week then.'

'No, no,' said Duncan, 'I've got what I came for.'

'MacAllister?'

'Aye. Clear as day. Car stops just up the street, she jumps out, sees the cordon around Carducci's place and jumps straight back in again.'

'Was she driving?' said Munro.

'No. She's the passenger. It's a taxi.'

'Can you make out who?'

'Better than that,' said Duncan. 'It's a Kestrel. Index: Sierra Golf One Four Oscar Juliet Yankee.'

* * *

Dabbing his face with a neatly pressed handkerchief, Munro followed West into the taxi office and nodded politely as Beth, craning her neck to peer through the window, greeted them with a smile.

'Inspector,' she said, 'I must say, you're looking better since the last time we met. Your skin's more, well, it's more skin colour.'

'You're too kind,' said Munro. 'Listen, we need a word with Jazz, would you mind shouting him for us?'

'Sorry. He's not here.'

'Know when he's back?' said West.

'Not today, I shouldn't think. We were down two drivers yesterday so he filled in. Probably putting his feet up, I imagine.'

'Have you got an address, please?' said West. 'I'm sure he won't mind if we drop by.'

'I have, indeed,' said Beth. 'It's Hawkhill Avenue, down by the racecourse. Number twenty-nine.'

'Thanking you,' said Munro. 'Oh, we need to check who was driving one of your cars yesterday, can you do that for me, Beth?'

'Aye, but not just now, Inspector. I'm in the middle of the rota. Can I do it for you later?'

'Nae bother. We'll drop by on our way back.'

* * *

A chubby, middle-aged lady wrapped in a pink towelling robe – her sodden, pitch-black hair scraped back in a pony tail – opened the door to the sandstone semi, raised her hands to her face and instinctively took a step back.

'Aletta Banerjee?' said West, holding up her warrant card.

'Oh, my God, what's happened?' said Aletta, her hazel eyes brimming with fear. 'Has there been an accident?'

'Excuse me?'

'An accident?'

'No,' said West, with a reassuring smile, 'honestly, there's nothing to worry about.'

'Thank Christ for that. I thought the police only knocked the door when they had bad news.

'Not always,' said Munro, 'but we've no bad news, I promise. We just need a word with Jazz.'

'Och, that's a relief,' said Aletta, 'for a minute there, I thought… is this about that stolen car you found in our yard?'

'You know about that?'

'Aye, of course. Jazz tells me everything. He said it was like something off the telly, with folk going over it, looking for clues and that.'

'I suppose it was,' said West, peering past Aletta and glancing down the hall. 'So, is he in?'

'Afraid not.'

'When do you expect him back?'

'No idea. I've not seen him since yesterday. He left to do an airport run first thing, and he had a full day ahead of him after that.'

'So, you've not seen him since yesterday?' said Munro. 'Are you not a wee bit concerned about that?'

'No. That man works like a dog, bless him, and knowing what he's like, he probably hit the pub with my brother when he finished and had one too many. They'll be sleeping it off round at his.'

'Okay, no worries,' said West, 'do you have an address? For your brother?'

'Och, let's not bother the man,' said Munro chipping in, 'there's no sense in talking to him if his head's in the fog. We'll call back later this evening, Mrs Banerjee, if that's okay with you?'

'Aye, no bother,' said Aletta. 'I'll say you've been asking for him.'

* * *

West flipped down the visor and, one hand on the steering wheel, chewed on her lower lip as she stared pensively down the street.

'What's up, lassie?' said Munro as he fastened his safety belt.

'Sunglasses,' said West.

'I've left them behind.'

'No. Sunglasses. The table in the hallway.'

'You're havering, again.'

'Banerjee's place. Just now. There was the telephone, a note pad, a pen, a small vase and a pair of sunglasses. Ray-Bans.'

'So?'

'Can you really see that woman wearing Wayfarers?'

'Each to their own.'

'No. Trust me,' said West, tenaciously. 'Call it female intuition but there's no way she'd wear them. They wouldn't suit her. But I know someone who would. Clare MacAllister.'

'Are you suggesting MacAllister is somehow in cahoots with Jazz?'

'Why not? She owns a pair exactly like that and in all the time we spoke to her, right from the moment she was nicked first time round, she hardly ever took them off. Remember?'

'Och, come on, Charlie, that's a wee bit tenuous, even for you. If they're not Aletta's, they must belong to Jazz, or a friend.'

'Give me strength, you're suffering from wood and trees syndrome. Look, they work together, right? The Golf was dumped in Kestrel's yard, right? And we know MacAllister was driving it, right? We've even got her on film. No. Something's bugging me about this. Big time.'

'Is your instinct kicking in, lassie?'

'It's booting me in the head, Jimbo,' said West as she started the engine. 'It's booting me in the head.'

* * *

'Back so soon, Inspector?' said Beth, apologetically. 'I'm sorry but I'm not ready yet.'

'We are,' said West, curtly. 'Jazz. He did an airport run yesterday. Is that right?'

'Aye, that's right.'

'And he was out all day?'

'Pretty much.'

'Okay, we need to know which car he was using. Is that easy to check?'

'Aye,' said Beth, huffing at the inconvenience, 'it's all logged down, just bear with me a moment. Och, would you look at that, he took the hoopty.'

'Come again?'

'The hoopty. The banger. The oldest one in the fleet. Will you be wanting the registration?'

'We will,' said Munro.

'SG14 OJY'

West spun to face Munro.

'Instinct,' she said, trying not to gloat. 'He wasn't on an airport run at all. He was the one who drove MacAllister to Kirkmichael.'

'Beth,' said Munro, glaring at West as he held out his hand, 'we need the keys to the yard and the spare for that car.'

'Oh, I'm not sure I can do that, Inspector, I should check with…'

'Now!'

* * *

The Prius, deftly parked with its rear to the wall, appeared, upon closer inspection, to be utterly unremarkable.

'Nothing here,' said Munro as he peered through the window.

'There wouldn't be, would there?' said West. 'If anything, *it*, whatever *it* is, would be hidden away. Wouldn't it?'

Munro, tickled by West's new-found confidence and her blossoming sense of sarcasm, stood to one side, smiling as she popped open the boot.

'Oh, dear,' he said, shaking his head as a lifeless Jazz, trussed hand and foot like a suckling pig ready for the roast, gazed up at him. 'He'll not be playing the trumpet again, that's for sure.'

West snapped on a pair of gloves and leaned cautiously into the boot.

'No lesions or burns to his wrists or ankles,' she said, as she prodded around the braided, yellow tow rope binding his limbs, 'so he didn't struggle. He was a goner before they tied him up.'

'They?'

'Different knots to the hands and feet.'

'Very good, Charlie. I'm impressed. What else?'

'No obvious injuries,' she said, 'he may as well have died in his sleep.'

'If he did, he was having a nightmare,' said Munro. 'You'd best come round this side and take a look at his face.'

West, grinning like the Cheshire Cat, nipped around the car and stood next to Munro.

'Cripes,' she said, struck by his twisted, pained expression. 'Scary.'

'Remind you of anyone?'

'Yeah. Angus Buchanan. In the back of Dubrowski's cab.'

'Indeed. We seem to have a monopoly on finding folk who refuse to pay their fare. Either way, I'll wager once they've had a rummage around his innards, they'll find a fair smattering of meth. Enough to induce a stroke and a cardiac. Just like Buchanan.'

'Okay,' said West, pulling her phone from her belt, 'I'll get Duncan over and ask him to get this sorted.'

Munro, eyes glued to the dormant Jazz, stood motionless for a moment and raised his hand, hesitating as his brain cranked into overdrive.

'Call Dougal first,' he said firmly. 'We need a warrant. Now. For Jazz's place. Tell him we've no time to go through the Fiscal, this is urgent, he's to go straight to the JP, understood?'

'Loud and clear,' said West, slightly confused. 'Silly question, I know, but… why?'

'Och, come on, lassie, now you're letting yourself down! Look, if Jazz was in cahoots with anyone, it's not going to be MacAllister, is it? Why deal with the monkey when Gundersen's the organ grinder? And mark my words, if Gundersen's involved, then so are drugs.'

'Okay, so we need to take a good look around before anyone has a chance to dump whatever it is we're looking for?'

'Hallelujah, she's got it. Oh, we'll need a Family Liaison Officer, too. This is going to knock his wife for six.'

* * *

West, incapable of standing still whilst talking on the phone, wandered around the yard before bounding back to Munro who, doubled-over the boot, was scrutinising the corpse with the diligence of a master forger inspecting his own handiwork.

'Sorted,' she said. 'Dougal's on the case and Duncan's on his way over. What're you looking at?'

'Unless Jazz was having gender issues,' said Munro, without looking up, 'I'd say he was up to no good before he slipped this mortal coil.'

'Now, who's havering?'

'Lipstick, Charlie. On his neck. And there's a wee smudge on the corner of his mouth, too.'

'Naughty boy, let's have a look,' said West, as she nudged Munro aside. 'Ooh, it's a sort of plummy colour. Tell you one thing, Jimbo, that doesn't belong to his wife.'

'Obviously. He's not been home.'

'Oh, yeah. But what I meant was…'

'Don't tell me. MacAllister.'

* * *

West, already buzzing due to the amount of adrenaline coursing through her veins rather than the usual mix of brown sauce and bacon fat, jumped back as the black Audi A4, its tail-end flailing like a fish out of water, screeched into the yard and headed straight for Munro, before careering to a heart-stopping halt inches from his legs.

'Came as quick as I could,' said Duncan, grinning as he leapt from the car.

'So I see,' said Munro, clearly unimpressed, 'but this is Police Scotland, laddie, not Hawaii Five-O. You'd do well to remember that.'

'Sorry, chief. So, what's happening?'

'It's Jazz,' said West, nodding towards the taxi, 'he's having a lie down in the boot.'

'Oh dear. Not another one?'

'Aye, and knowing my luck,' said Munro, 'he'll not be the last. Okay, Duncan, you're to remain here until forensics are done, got that? And while they're keeping themselves busy, check with the office, find out if Jazz had exclusive rights to this vehicle or if anyone else used it within the last three days.'

'Roger that, chief.'

'Also, Jazz has a key to this yard. Check his pockets and get it dusted. It's a long shot but it might let us know if he lent it to anyone. We're away to his house just now. Charlie's kindly volunteered to break the bad news to his wife.'

'Thanks a bunch,' said West. She stormed towards the car, snatching her phone as Munro trailed lamely in her wake.

'Dougal?'

'You're good to go, miss. Warrant's all sorted and the FLO will meet you there.'

'Nice one, Dougal. Thanks.'

'There's something else you both should hear.'

'Two ticks,' said West as she waited for Munro to shut the door, 'just waiting for the old man to buckle up. Okay, what have you got?'

'It's about Rietveld.'

'Och, Dougal, we dinnae have time for that,' said Munro, 'we're a hurry.'

'Trust me, sir, you'll regret it if you don't.'

'Very well,' he said, raising his eyebrows, 'quick as you can.'

'Okay,' said Dougal, 'you remember Rietveld was down as a no-show for the flight he booked? Well, I've gone through the passenger lists for all the other flights that day, and he's not on any of them…'

'For goodness sake, laddie, I'm losing the will to live, here.'

'…but there was someone else travelling on the flight he missed. Lars Gundersen.'

West flinched and drew a short, sharp breath as a stony-faced Munro sat staring vacuously into space.

'I knew it,' he said, heaving a sigh.

'Knew what?'

'I knew I should have stayed in Carsethorn. Now we've got the Flying Dutchman to deal with, as well as Erik the Red.'

'Not necessarily,' said West, trying to ease the tension, 'I mean, we don't know for certain yet that the two of them are connected. Maybe it was just, you know…'

'If you say coincidence, lassie, I really will head back to Carsethorn.'

'Well, what the hell is Rietveld doing with Gundersen, anyway? It simply doesn't make sense.'

'Really?' said Munro as he lowered the window and loosened his tie. 'A drug dealer who makes a fortune from selling meth gets involved with a chap who's passing himself off as a solicitor, with a track record in laundering the proceeds of stolen assets, and you think it doesnae make any sense?'

'Well, if you put it like that,' said West, 'I suppose there's an outside chance their relationship could be mutually beneficial. So. What now?'

Munro frowned and glanced towards the phone.

'Dougal, are you still there?' he said.

'Sir.'

'Okay, listen, I need to know if Gundersen's ever been to Eindhoven before, or if this was a one-off. Get your pal, Klassen, to check with immigration. Do the same with Rietveld and see if he's ever been to Oslo. That could be where he met Gundersen. Got that?'

'Leave it to me.'

'Not so fast. Dig out everything we have on Remo Carducci and Angus Buchanan from Companies House and their accountants. We need to know if Rietveld represented them in any way, then get yourself over to Hawkhill Avenue.'

'Got to hand it you, Jimbo,' said West as they pulled away, 'it would've taken me ages to figure that out.'

'Dinnae get your hopes up, lassie. If Rietveld is involved with Gundersen, and if Gundersen made the flight but Rietveld didn't, then he's probably dead meat.'

Chapter 13

Cursing the lack of shelter on the treeless Hawkhill Avenue, West – combining initiative with a liberal dose of bare-faced cheek – reversed into the neighbour's drive and killed the engine, thankful for the shade of their ivy-clad carport.

'Officially,' said Munro with a wry smile, 'you're trespassing.'

'I know, but that's a civil offence,' said West, 'so what are they going to do about it?'

'Well, some folk are tetchy about that kind of thing, lassie. You could find yourself blocked in.'

'Then that would be a criminal offence – causing an obstruction and denial of access to a public highway and, being a cop, I can nick them straight away. It's a win-win for the perp.'

'Perhaps you'd like to explain that to her,' said Munro, pointing out the woman in a fleece top and carrying a shoulder bag, locking the green Nissan Micra on the opposite side of the road and heading towards them.

'Oh, blimey, that's all I need,' said West. 'I'll just say we were turning around. No harm done.'

Munro smiled apologetically as the tender-faced, young lady stopped by his door and bent forward.

'DI Munro?' she said, her voice as soft as velvet. 'And DS West?'

'Present and correct, lassie. And you must be…?'

'PC Sue Hamilton. I'm the Family Liaison Officer.'

'Of course you are. Jump in, Sue, we're just waiting for young Dougal to arrive.'

'That's DC McCrae,' said West, 'he shouldn't be long.'

'No worries. Perhaps you'd like to fill me in while we wait?'

'As much as I can,' said West, swivelling in her seat, 'can't say too much, though, know what I mean?'

'Of course.'

'Right, Jasminder Banerjee, otherwise known as Jazz, owner of Kestrel Cars, found dead in the boot of one of his own taxis earlier this morning. He'll be out of bounds until they've completed a post-mortem. Suspected murder, but keep that under your hat, okay?'

'Okay.'

'All his wife needs to know at this stage, is that he's dead, and we'll find out why in due course.'

'No problem,' said Sue, 'is there anything you need to know? Anything I should be asking her?'

'Yup. Sure is,' said West. 'See what you can find out about her husband's whereabouts these last few days. What hours he was working, if there was a change to his normal pattern, coming home late, that kind of thing.'

'Okay.'

'And ask about his mates. See if he'd met anyone new or started drinking in a different pub, maybe.'

'I'll do my best,' Sue said in her best bedside manner.

'Her name's Aletta,' said Munro, 'and it'll come as no surprise to someone like yourself that she's going to take this pretty hard. Thing is, Sue, we've a warrant to search the premises and I'm not in the mood for upsetting her further, so I'll give you fifteen minutes, then you're to take her off, is that okay?'

'Aye, I can do that,' said Sue, 'if she agrees, that is. I can't force her, though, you know that, don't you?'

'Yeah, we know,' said West. 'If she won't go, I'll have a word.'

'Here comes Dougal,' said Munro, as the whining pitch of a scooter on full throttle grew louder and louder.

'And there goes Dougal,' said West, as something shot past them in a blur.

* * *

Unlike the lady they'd inadvertently dragged from the shower a few hours earlier, Aletta – wearing a bright, orange dress with make-up to match – looked as radiant as summer itself.

'He's still not back,' she said, smiling as though she'd swallowed the sun, 'you should have taken Robbie's address the last time you called, saved yourself a trip.'

'Oh, we'll not be needing it now,' said Munro, with the subtlest of smiles.

'You found him, then? Och, no wonder you're detectives. Still blootered, no doubt?'

'No, no. Sober as a judge, actually. Stone cold sober, you might say.'

Aletta dropped the smile and fixed PC Hamilton with a worried gaze.

'You weren't here this morning,' she said, disconcerted by her presence, 'who are you?'

'My name's Sue. I'm a Family Liaison Officer.'

'A family…? I've seen them on the telly, they only… oh, Jesus.'

'Shall we go inside, Aletta?' said West, as she eased open the door. 'It's a bit more private in there.'

* * *

Munro retired to the shelter of the carport and perched himself on the bonnet of the Toyota as Dougal, scanning the houses for door numbers, pootled towards him.

'I went too far,' he said, as he hung his helmet on the wing mirror, 'had to come back down again.'

'I noticed,' said Munro. 'Are you not familiar with the phrase "twenty's plenty"?'

'I am, aye, but is this not an emergency?'

'It is not.'

'Honest mistake then.'

'You're getting as bad as Charlie,' said Munro, with a smirk.

'Where is she?'

'Inside. Breaking the bad news with the FLO.'

'Are you not joining her?'

'No, no. Three's a crowd. They'll be leaving soon enough, then we can go inside.'

'Okay,' said Dougal, 'just to let you know, I emailed Klassen and gave him the heads-up on Rietveld. I said there may be a body at the address in Oirschot.'

'Let's hope that there is, it'll certainly make our life a lot easier. Have you not heard back from the lab yet?'

'Sometime today, apparently. But I'm not holding my breath.'

* * *

A solemn-faced Munro watched as an inconsolable Aletta – her eyes black with tear-stained mascara – clung to PC Hamilton as she crossed the street with the agility of an octogenarian suffering from osteoporosis.

'Right, that's them away,' he said morosely, as he ambled over to West, waiting on the doorstep. 'No need to ask how she took it.'

'Gutted,' said West. 'That Gundersen's got a lot to answer for.'

'Aye, right enough, but he'll get what's coming to him. Eventually.'

'Will he hell,' said West, venomously. 'Even if we do nail him, he'll still be out before teatime. I'd like to wring his bloody neck and squeeze every last drop of…'

'Dear, dear, dear,' said Munro, 'and there was I thinking that after your spiritual retreat you'd learned the power of forgiveness, Charlie.'

'Are you winding me up?'

'Do you not believe in karma? It's a lot less messy.'

'No, Jimbo. I'm rapidly becoming a believer in the law of talion.'

'I've a leaflet at home about anger management. Remind me to pass it on to you. So, where are they headed?'

'They're off to see her brother, Robbie. He'll be in for a shock too.'

'No doubt about that, Charlie. No doubt at all. Did you ask her about the sunglasses?'

'Yup. Said she hadn't even noticed them. Reckons they must belong to Jazz, or someone left them in the back of his taxi.'

'That's not all they left. And MacAllister's not been here?'

'Never. Not so far as she knows.'

* * *

Furnished with a three-piece suite, a coffee table, and an obtrusively large television which sat like a shrine to banality in the bay window, the lounge – devoid of books, pictures and the usual keepsakes that accumulate over the years – had about as much charm as the departure lounge of a small provincial airport.

'They're not one for clutter, are they?' said Munro, curling his lip at the plastic lilies in the boarded-up fireplace.

'Not everyone likes to live surrounded by tat, Jimbo,' said West as she made herself at home on the sofa. 'I believe it's called *feng shui.*'

'Really? I thought it was Ikea.'

'If you two have quite finished,' said Dougal, standing by the door like the uninvited guest at a house-warming, 'would someone mind telling me why we're here?'

'Sorry,' said West, 'it's Jazz. We're pretty damned certain he was force-fed an unhealthy dose of meth, which is why he ended up in the same state as Angus Buchanan.'

'Okay.'

'And we've a hunch that he was peddling it for Gundersen, probably out of his taxi.'

'So, you reckon he's got a stash about the place?'

'We're not positive,' said Munro, 'but, aye, it's a possibility. If he has, it'll not be much, enough for a few days, maybe, which makes it easier to hide, and harder to find. So, Charlie, you start down here, then the kitchen – under the cupboards, behind the drawers, in the cereal boxes. Dougal, you and me, upstairs.'

* * *

Dougal, having exhausted the minimal amount of possible hiding places in the bathroom – from the toilet cistern and the bath panel, to the air vent and the lamp shade – joined Munro in the bedroom.

'Nothing there, sir,' he said. 'How about you? Any luck?'

'No,' said Munro, despondently. 'I've been through everything – wardrobe, chest of drawers, divan, even the pillow cases.'

'Well, it was only a hunch, they don't always pay off.'

'Mine do, laddie. Rest assured. Mine do. Right, downstairs. Let's start again.'

* * *

Munro stood in the centre of the lounge, one hand behind his back, and slowly turned full circle, frowning as he meticulously scoured the room from top to bottom, looking for signs that the carpet may have been lifted, the skirting removed, or even a plug point capped off.

'This is actually quite a nice house,' said Dougal, 'if you can see past the décor, that is. Or should I say, the lack of it.'

'I'm inclined to agree,' said Munro, only half listening.

'Aye. Be better with proper sash windows, though, not those plastic jobbies. And if they opened up the fire, this place would be nice and toasty in the winter.'

Munro froze, glanced at Dougal, and stepped towards the fireplace, easing himself down to the hearth and slowly running his index finger around the edge of the piece of wood sealing off the firebox.

'Upstairs. Bedroom,' he said, smiling as he made for the door.

* * *

Munro positioned himself by the window and pointed at the fireplace.

'Look at that and tell me what you see,' he said. 'Take your time, laddie, consider the detail, and no facetious remarks.'

'Okay, said Dougal, nervously, as he squatted by the bed. 'Tiled surround. Cast iron grate. Ceramic vase. Not sure what kind of flowers these are though.'

'Tulips. Go On.'

Dougal swallowed hard as he struggled to find anything else to mention, wary that his next comment may be deemed flippant at best.

'It's sealed off, like the one downstairs. Probably plywood, white finish. Held on with one, two, three, four, five, six screws. Silver.'

'And how do you know they're silver, laddie?'

'Well, it's obvious, isn't it?' said Dougal, fearing he was falling for a trap. 'You can see for yourself, the paint's chipped off.'

Munro, saying nothing, smiled as he leant against the window and waited.

'The paint's chipped off!'

'Hallelujah,' said Munro. 'Have you got your fancy penknife with you?'

Dougal, hands trembling with excitement, unscrewed the panel and paused as it fell it away.

'There's no beasties back here, are there?' he said, glancing over his shoulder.

'Och, maybe a rat or two, but they'll be more scared of you than you are of them.'

'I wouldn't be so sure about that,' said Dougal as he removed the panel and retrieved a soft package the size of a small shoebox wrapped in a black, plastic bin bag and sealed with copious amounts of masking tape.'

'What are you waiting for?' said Munro. 'You're the one with the knife.'

Dougal made a small incision, ripped open the plastic and turned to Munro, grinning as though he'd discovered the holy grail.

'Well done, laddie. Full marks for initiative.'

'Me? I've not done anything. You were the one who…'

'Och, utter tosh. You're too modest by far, Dougal. Too modest, by far. Call the FLO, tell her we need to question Aletta, just as soon as she's ready.'

* * *

West, slumped on the sofa with a face as long as a camel's snout, barely moved as Munro, looking unusually smug, sauntered into the room.

'What are you looking so happy about?' she said.

'Och, you're confusing me with somebody else, lassie. I'm not happy unless I'm being miserable. Are you okay? You look a wee bit… peaky.'

'Me? I'm fine. Why?'

'Have you not seen the time?'

'Yeah, what of it?'

'And you're not hungry?'

'Thin ice, Jimbo,' said West, as Dougal, beaming from ear to ear, joined them. 'Oh, God, not you as well. Why are you grinning like a halfwit?'

'No reason,' said Dougal as he produced the package from behind his back, 'just found a few hundred tabs, that's all. In the bedroom.'

'Tablets? I thought they were dealing meth?'

'Perhaps they're for Aletta,' said Munro, 'maybe she's prone to headaches.'

'You are unbelievable.'

'Okay, let's be serious for a moment. This now proves that Jazz, one way or another, was involved with Gundersen, okay? But, unless we can round up a few junkies who'll testify to it, we cannae prove that he was actually selling the stuff.'

'Right enough,' said Dougal, 'but their collusion would explain why Jazz was ferrying MacAllister around like a salaried chauffeur.'

'Well, that's good, isn't it?' said West, 'I mean, we're making progress.'

'Aye, but one question remains, Charlie,' said Munro, 'where the hell is MacAllister?'

'I'll ponder that one later. We off?'

'Aye,' said Munro, 'we are. Dougal, one thing before you go, get this place sealed off and arrange for the Tyveks to give it the once over. We'll see you back at the office.'

Chapter 14

Munro sat with his head in his hands, gazing intently at the flow chart he'd scrawled on a scrappy piece of A4 paper, featuring the names of those involved – Anita and Remo Carducci, Angus Buchanan, Jazz Banerjee and Clare MacAllister – all linking directly back to Lars Gundersen, with a secondary link connecting MacAllister to Jazz and Anita Carducci. The only name out on its own was Lucas Rietveld. He flinched, irritated by the sound of West's phone, as he circled it again and again.

'Duncan,' West said softly, trying not to break the silence, 'how's it going?'

'Just finishing up, miss. The body's away and the SOCOs are packing up. All we have to do is secure the yard and we're all done. Oh, and that Beth woman's in a real state, I had to get uniform to take her home.'

'Okay, excellent. Cheers, Duncan.'

'Anything else I should be doing?'

'No, not really,' said West, stifling a yawn. 'Oh yeah, actually there is. Can you give Dougal a hand? Remember he sent you the case files on Carducci and Buchanan?'

'Oh aye,' said Duncan. 'Not exactly light reading, is it?'

'No, but I need you to go through them and see if Rietveld's name pops up anywhere. See if he had any dealings with them, maybe through their accountants.'

'Roger that, miss. I'll take a look as soon as I get back to Dumfries and give you a bell if I find anything.'

'One more thing, can you take a look around Rietveld's gaff at some point. He rents a house on Braemar Square. See if anything turns up.'

* * *

Munro set down his pen and stretched his one good arm.

'Good call, Charlie,' he said, 'wee Dougal's already doing the work of three men.'

'I know, he's a diamond,' said West as she swung her legs onto the desk and leaned back, 'you're quite fond of him, aren't you?'

'It's more admiration, lassie. He's already shown what he's capable of. The lad deserves a chance to prove his worth once and for all.'

'So you're thinking promotion?'

'That's not for me to say, I'm just helping out, remember?'

'Leave it with me then,' said West, 'the only thing is, I don't think they'll see the point of having two DSs in the same department, and it'd be a shame to lose him.'

'Och, someone will have to have a word with DCI Elliot then. Dougal's not the only who deserves a step up the ladder.'

'DI West? Not sure about that. Fancy a cuppa?'

'No, no. It's too late for tea,' said Munro, rubbing his forehead. 'I'm in need of something a wee bit more medicinal.'

'Are you alright? You look bothered.'

'I am. It's this Rietveld fellow. See here, Charlie, we know he's probably, and I mean *probably*, involved with

Gundersen, okay? The question still remains, how and why?'

'Well, Duncan's looking into that. Maybe there's…'

'No, no, no!' said Munro, impatiently. 'He's wasting his time. Look, with a name like Rietveld, do you not think we'd have recognised it if he'd been involved with Carducci and Buchanan in the first place?'

'Well, yeah. Maybe. But we could've missed it.'

'No, Charlie. No, we did not.'

* * *

West glanced up as Dougal, looking more than a little flustered, flew through the door and headed straight for his desk.

'You two look happy,' he said as he woke his computers and sat down, 'is everything okay?'

'We're fine. How about you?'

'Aye, all good,' said Dougal, checking his watch. 'The FLO says Aletta's beside herself with grief. She's stopping with her brother so I told her to bring her in, first thing.'

'Fair enough,' said West. 'It's a bit late to be sticking her under the spotlight, anyway. Considering what she's been through.'

Munro, looking as though he'd inadvertently swallowed a wasabi-coated peanut, picked up his pen and began tapping it rhythmically on the desk.

'Dougal,' he said, tossing the pen to one side, 'what do you know about this Reitveld fellow?'

'Only what I've told you. Why?'

'He's not in the same mould as the others. He's too clever by half.'

'Maybe that's exactly why he's involved.'

'So he can screw Gundersen?' said West. 'Take him for everything he's got?'

'No,' said Munro, 'that's not it.'

'Why not? He may as well have *greed is good* tattooed on his arm.'

'No. It's not that simple, trust me. There has to be another link. Dougal, that lassie who knows the priest, Rietveld's girlfriend, what's her name again?'

'Alison Kennedy.'

'Aye. Find out everything you can about her.'

'Alison Kennedy?' said Dougal, flabbergasted. 'Are you joking me?'

'See if you can find a link between her and any of the others. Start with Gundersen.'

'Och, with all due respect, sir, we'll be on a hiding to nothing, there. The man's an enigma, you know that. Even the Norwegian authorities have nothing on him. And Alison Kennedy, she's… well, come on, she runs the care home.'

'I want to know if she's ever been to Oslo.'

'Sir.'

'And contact your pals in the Hordaland District, tell them we need records of births, marriages and deaths of every single person called Lars Gundersen born in Oslo between fifty and sixty years ago. Understood?'

'Aye,' said Dougal, reluctantly. 'Understood. You'll not mind if I start that in the morning, only it's getting late.'

'Late?' said Munro. 'Since when have you been bothered by *late*?'

'Since now.'

'What are you up to?' said West, as Dougal's cheeks began to flush. 'You sly dog, you've got a date, haven't you?'

'No, it's just… yes. Kind of. But it's nothing serious. I mean…'

'On you go, Dougal,' said Munro with a smirk. 'Punctuality is the politeness of kings.'

'Thanks. I'll just check the email, then that's me away.'

'I can do that,' said West, 'don't keep the poor girl waiting.'

'You're alright, miss, this'll only take... uh-oh. We've got four. From the lab.'

'Four?' said Munro. 'Good grief, it's famine or feast with those chaps.'

Dougal frowned as his eyes flashed hurriedly across the screen.

'Okay,' he said, shifting excitedly in his seat, 'here we go. They've got a match for the prints they lifted from the stuff I took from Rietveld's office...'

'Brilliant!' said West.

'...as yet, unidentified.'

'What? If they're unidentified, who on earth did they match him to?'

'Wait for it... a set of prints taken from a VW Golf on the premises of Kestrel Cars. Smith Street.'

A moment's silence descended on the room as Munro, raising his hand, locked eyes with West.

'Okay,' he said, 'so we now we know for definite that Rietveld's mixed up with Gundersen and, by association, MacAllister as well.'

'Excellent!' said West, slapping her thigh.

'I'd like to know what your definition of excellent is, Charlie,' said Munro, shaking his head, 'because from where I'm sitting, we have three suspects in cahoots with each other and no idea where a single one of them is.'

'Two words,' said West. 'Rain. Parade.'

'Okay,' said Dougal, 'the other three emails relate to the Golf. Let's see... prints – the only match is to Clare MacAllister. All the others, also as yet unidentified. The DNA samples they took from the drinking straw... also a match to MacAllister. And that's it, apart from the hair samples...'

'Come on,' said West, 'tell me they match someone.'

'Not someone, miss,' said Dougal, sighing as he glanced furtively across the desk. 'Something.'

'Come again?'

'It's a modacrylic fibre composed of acrylonitrate and vinyl chloride.'

'What?'

'It's synthetic. Made in Japan.'

'You mean, it's a bloody wig?'

Munro walked to the window, leaned on the sill and stared pensively down at the deserted supermarket car park below.

'I don't believe it!' said West, hollering as she ruffled her hair. 'No wonder we can't bloody find them, they're all dressing up like Coco the bleeding Clown! God only knows what MacAllister looks like right now, probably parading around like…'

'Haud yer wheesht, lassie!'

Munro lowered his voice and spoke without turning.

'Dougal,' he said quietly. 'Send those fingerprints to your pals in Oslo and Eindhoven, quick as you can. Then take yourself off, you'll not forgive yourself if you're late. And neither will she.'

'Sir. That's me done then.'

'And one last thing before you go,' said Munro, as he turned to face them, one corner of his mouth raised in a knowing smile, 'we can forget about trying to establish a connection between The Flying Dutchman and Lars Gundersen.'

'What? I don't follow,' said Dougal, 'we've just got proof that they were in the Golf together.'

'Rietveld wasnae travelling with Lars Gundersen, laddie. He is Lars Gundersen.'

Chapter 15

West, berating herself for missing what appeared to be the blindingly obvious link between the hair samples and the fingerprints, and Gundersen and Rietveld, sat in the silence of the office with her arms folded, staring at the back of Munro's head as he gazed out across the rooftops at the fading amber twilight.

'Oi, Jimbo,' she said, softly. 'What size shoes do you take?'

'What? Why?'

'Because, come hell or high water, there's no way I'm going to fill them.'

'Utter tosh,' said Munro, 'of course you will, lassie. You're forgetting, I've a thirty-year head start on you. You'll catch up.'

'I admire your confidence.'

'Let's hope it's not misplaced. Now, make a note, mental or otherwise, you need to gather everything you possibly can on Gundersen's alter-ego. Dougal's following up with that Kennedy woman, so you need to talk to the wee lassie who works with him and anyone at the care home who may have had dealings with him. And put a rocket up the arse of our friends in Eindhoven. If anyone's got anything on him, it'll be them.'

'Anything else?'

'Issue another APW,' said Munro, 'including the railway stations. We cannae afford to let him slip the net again. Understood?'

'Yes, boss.'

'Very funny. Now, assuming my room at your fancy apartment is still available, I suggest we check it's free from intruders.'

'No rush,' said West, 'we'll get there, eventually.'

'Eventually? You're becoming very lackadaisical in your dotage, lassie. What's keeping you?'

'Hunger,' said West as she pulled on her coat. 'Come on. Few drinks, a couple of steaks and a mountain of chips. My treat.'

* * *

Comfortable in the familiar surroundings of the Ayrshire and Galloway Hotel, West – finally realising adrenaline was no substitute for a decent lunch – settled back, pushed the menu to one side and waved frantically at the waitress in a desperate bid to grab her attention.

'I could eat a horse,' she said, licking her lips.

'Och, if I'd have known that,' said Munro, 'we could've gone to that French restaurant across the street.'

Despite her best efforts, West could not control her laughter as the waitress, disappointed that she'd missed out on the joke, greeted them with a dour smile.

'Glad to see someone's enjoying themselves,' she said wearily. 'What can I get you?'

'Two rib-eyes, please,' said West, 'done to a crisp. As many chips as you can fit on the plate, a vodka and orange, and a large, single malt.'

'I wonder how Dougal's getting on,' said Munro, as the waitress trudged towards the bar, 'as I recall, his last dalliance wasnae up to much.'

'I know. Poor bloke, she ate him alive. Almost. He needs to find someone with similar interests.'

'Aye, a member of the Temperance Society with a fondness for monkfish and a working knowledge of the internal combustion engine.'

'You're cruel,' said West, reaching for her phone. 'Sorry, not being rude but I'd better see who this is. Crap, it's the ACR.'

Munro instinctively reached for his coat as West took the call.

'DS West. Go ahead, control.'

'Miss. Female, IC1, answering the description of Clare MacAllister seen heading south along Tams Brig towards Allison Street.'

'What? MacAllister?'

'Aye, an off-duty Special called it in. He's following on foot. Shall we engage?'

'No, no, no! Do not approach, under any circumstances, suspect may be dangerous. Hold the line. Jimbo – Tams Brig, where the hell is that?'

'Newton on Ayr,' said Munro, 'five minutes. Two if you put your foot down.'

'Control, tell your man to back off, I mean, right off. We're on our way.'

'Do you require assistance, DS West?'

'Negative,' said West, smiling as they raced for the door. 'Come on, Jimbo. I know where she's going!'

'Well, dinnae keep it to yourself, lassie.'

'She's heading for Glebe Crescent. And that's where Aletta's brother lives.'

* * *

West parked under the glow of a street lamp, taken aback by the sight of the faceless, two storey villas dotted about the crescent which, even under cover of darkness, resembled the housing equivalent of a supermarket's budget range of groceries.

'Blimey, this is a step down from Hawkhill Avenue,' she said. 'Not exactly brimming with character, is it?'

'Hardly surprising,' said Munro. 'Local authorities aren't renowned for spending, lassie, you should know that. In fact, they cut so many corners, it's a wonder these houses aren't round. Which one's his?'

West pointed to the ground floor flat directly opposite.

'There,' she said, 'with the lights on.'

* * *

West rang the bell and took a step back as a shadowy figure approached the door, opening it just enough to peek through.

'Can I help?' said the swarthy Indian man, frowning suspiciously.

'You must be Robbie.'

'Who's asking?'

'DS West. DI Munro. Is PC Hamilton here?'

'She's gone to fetch us some supper.'

'Alright for some,' said Munro under his breath.

'And Aletta?'

'She's resting.'

'Good,' said West. 'And how about Clare MacAllister?'

'Clare? What would Clare be doing here?'

'Well, I assume, as you work together, she's come to offer her condolences.'

'She's not here,' said Robbie, brusquely, his attempt to close the door thwarted by Munro's plaster cast.

'I'd like to take your word for that,' he said, 'but I'm not convinced you're being entirely honest with us. We'll check for ourselves, if you don't mind.'

'You can whistle, pal. Unless you've a warrant, you're not coming in.'

'Well, I beg to differ,' said Munro, fixing him with a steely-blue gaze as West pulled the radio from her hip. 'See here, Robbie, we're in pursuit of a known criminal who we believe to be hiding on these premises. As such, we have the right to enter your house either with, or without, your consent. So, which is it to be?'

Relenting, Robbie pulled the door open wide.

'Sorry, Clare,' he said, as Munro and West focused on MacAllister, standing stock still in the hallway. 'I did my best.'

'Hello, Clare,' said West as she wiped her feet and stepped inside. 'You look different without your sunglasses.'

MacAllister, expecting a stand-off, stood with her legs akimbo and arms folded.

'I lost them,' she said, glowering.

'Shame. They're not cheap. I could tell you where they are, but I wouldn't want to embarrass you in front of Aletta.'

'You're all heart,' said MacAllister. 'Let's have it then, what are you here for?'

'Oh, not much,' said West, 'I just wanted to say, Clare MacAllister, I'm arresting you on suspicion of the murder of Anita Carducci...'

'What?'

'...possession of a stolen vehicle...'

'I don't believe this.'

'...and aiding and abetting Lars Gundersen, also known as Lucas Rietveld, in obtaining property by deception. You do not have to say anything but it may harm your defence if you do not mention when questioned, something you later rely on in court...'

'I've not done anything! Do you not get that?'

'...Anything you do say, may be given in evidence. Turn around, please, hands behind your back, I've got a lovely pair of bracelets for you to try on.'

'Hold on there!' said Robbie, flailing his arms as he grew more and more agitated. 'Did you not hear her! She just told you, she's not done anything!'

Munro stepped forward, forcing Robbie to the wall, and glared down at him.

'You listen to me, sonny,' he said. 'You've already lied to us once, any more from you and you'll be done for obstruction. Do I make myself clear?'

PC Hamilton, carrying a brown, paper carrier bag, ambled up the path as West frogmarched MacAllister to the car.

'Is everything okay?' she said, a look of consternation on her face.

'Dinnae take this the wrong way, lassie,' said Munro, scowling, 'but you are not to leave this house again, is that clear? Next time, use a delivery service.'

Chapter 16

Without her Wayfarers to hide behind, MacAllister, no stranger to the interview room, appeared uncharacteristically subdued as she sat, head bowed, fidgeting with her sleeves. West – half wishing she'd turned her phone off when they'd arrived at the restaurant – made herself comfortable and stabbed the voice recorder with her index finger.

'Okay,' she said, 'this is Detective Sergeant West. Also present is Detective Inspector James Munro, Constable Anderson and Miss Clare MacAllister. The time is 8:17pm. So, Clare, down to business – what was your relationship with Anita Carducci?'

'Pals.'

'Pals? Really? Did you bond over the death of her husband, Remo?'

'No.'

'No,' said West. 'Because you had an affair with him, didn't you? So, what brought you two closer together? Knitting?'

'Circumstances,' said MacAllister.

'Being?'

'I lost my job at the restaurant when Remo died. You know that.'

'So?'

'So, I got work at the taxi office and needed somewhere to stay close by. I wasn't going to travel all the way from Prestwick for a few lousy quid, now, was I?'

'And she offered you a room? Just like that?' said West. 'Despite everything that had gone before?'

'She's very forgiving, is Anita. We actually had a lot in common.'

'Like what?'

'Our taste in men,' said MacAllister, facetiously.

'So, why did you kill her?'

'I did no such thing.'

'But you admit you saw her body?' said West.

'I did. Aye.'

'And you did nothing about it?'

'No,' said MacAllister, sheepishly. 'I was too scared. I didn't want to get involved.'

'Involved with what?'

'Them. Whoever killed her.'

'And do you know who *they* are?'

'No idea. And I've no intention of finding out, either. Tommy…'

'Tomek Dubrowski?'

'Aye. He warned me about them after they'd paid him to take care of Angus Buchanan.'

'I see,' said West, 'nonetheless, despite the fact that you were *too scared*, you still went back to the house. Why?'

'I didn't go back, I told you. Not with Anita lying there.'

'Oh, come on, Clare,' said West, tiring of MacAllister's defiant attitude. 'We've got some very nice film of you jumping out of a Kestrel car and jumping back in again as soon as you'd spotted the cordon around the house. So, again, why did you go back?'

MacAllister paused as she cleared her throat.

'I forgot my necklace,' she said. 'I left it in the bedroom.'

'The main bedroom?' said Munro. 'At the front of the house?'

'Aye, that's the one I was using.'

'Hold on,' said West, 'Anita Carducci lets you, the woman who had an affair with her husband, sleep in their marital bed?'

'Her choice.'

'If that's the case,' said Munro, 'then why did we not find any of your clothes there?'

'I was living out of a bag. I hadn't moved in, it was just somewhere to kip.'

'Okay, but if you were so keen to get your necklace back,' said West, 'why didn't you go alone? Why did you wait for Jazz take you?'

'He offered. I wasn't going to turn down a lift, was I?'

'Did you tell him about Anita Carducci?'

'No. I just said I needed to pick something up and he said he'd run me there.'

'And afterwards? Where did you go afterwards?'

'He dropped me back at Robbie's,' said MacAllister. 'You can check, if you like.'

West sat back, folded her arms, and stared at MacAllister.

'You got on well, you two,' she said. 'You and Jazz?'

'Well enough. Aye.'

'Tell us about him.'

MacAllister frowned at the apparent absurdity of the question.

'What's there to tell?'

'I don't know, I'm asking you. Surely you must know something, I mean, since you two were having a fling, you must've shared something?'

'A fling? Me and Jazz?' said MacAllister, smiling nervously. 'Don't talk daft. We did no such thing.'

Munro, instigating a pause, slowly leaned forward, placed his elbows on the desk and clasped his hands beneath his chin.

'See here, Miss MacAllister,' he said, his voice tinged with a low, menacing air, 'you'd best be sure about that because when they do the post-mortem on Jazz, you know, after they've taken a wee knife, made an incision under his chin and sliced his throat open all the way down to the collarbone, once they've opened up his stomach and had a good rummage around to see what it was that killed him, they'll then take swabs from his body. From his mouth and his nether regions, and then they'll test them, and if we find any of your DNA in the samples…'

'I told you,' said MacAllister, 'there was nothing going on! Nothing at all!'

'Then perhaps,' said West, 'you'd care to explain why your sunglasses are at his house?'

MacAllister's face lit up like a six-year old learning she was off to Disneyland.

'Really? Brilliant!' she said. 'I must've left them in the taxi.'

'The one he was driving when he ran you to Carducci's?'

'Aye. Probably.'

'See, what I'm struggling with here, Miss MacAllister,' said Munro, 'is why Jazz would want to keep that a secret. Everyone thought he was doing an airport run that morning. Why would he lie about giving you a lift to the house?'

'Search me.'

'And you're adamant that you and he have nothing to hide?'

'Nothing at all.'

West stood up, pushed her chair beneath the desk and leaned against the wall.

'Did you know Jazz was acting as a runner for the nutters who killed Anita Carducci?' she said. 'Dealing as well, I imagine.'

'No. I did not.'

'You're positive?'

'Aye. If he was into drugs, then more fool him. It's a mug's game.'

'Pot and kettle,' said Munro with a wry smirk. 'Let's move on. Round two. You're quite a proficient driver, are you not, Miss MacAllister? What's your verdict on the Volkswagen Golf? Does she handle well?'

'Are you winding me up?'

'Just answer the question.'

'I wouldn't know,' said MacAllister. 'I've never driven one.'

'Then you must be suffering from amnesia,' said Munro. 'Here, allow me to jog your memory. For the benefit of the tape I am showing Clare MacAllister a still taken from the CCTV cameras outside the hospital that shows her behind the wheel of a white VW Golf, registration SF12 HLE.'

MacAllister slumped back without looking at the photo.

'Okay,' she said, sighing as she shifted uncomfortably in her seat. 'I might have driven one. Once.'

'And the chap in the passenger seat?'

'No idea. Jazz gave me the keys to the Golf, asked me to pick him up, take him to the hospital and wait. I assumed he had an appointment.'

'Aye, he did,' said Munro, smiling. 'He came to see me. Did he have a name, your passenger? What did you talk about?'

'Nothing. He never said a word the whole time he was with me.'

'Oh, the silent type, eh?' said West. 'That is convenient. So, where did you drop him when you left the hospital?'

'Braemar Square. On the corner.'

'And the car?'

'Jazz told me to park it in the yard when I'd finished.'

'Of course he did,' said Munro, cynically. 'Okay, final round. How long have you known Lucas Rietveld?'

'Who?' said MacAllister, glancing furtively towards the door.

'Lucas Rietveld.'

'Never heard of him.'

'Alright,' said West, 'let's try another. How about Lars Gundersen?'

MacAllister pursed her lips and shrugged her shoulders.

'Is that it then?' she said. 'Can I go now?'

'Go?' said West, feigning surprise. 'Nah, I don't think so. You see, Clare, I've still got hundreds of questions to ask you but, frankly, I'm hungry and now is not the time.'

'Are you joking me? Listen, I know my rights, you can't hold me here against my will.'

'Och, come, come, Miss MacAllister,' said Munro, as he stood, 'you're not telling me you've forgotten about our reward scheme, already? Let me remind you – you get your first twelve hours on the house, and after that, the less you say, the more you earn. We'll give you thirty-six, if we have to.'

'But you've not even charged me with anything!'

'Gosh, you're right,' said West, 'how remiss of us. Clare MacAllister, I am charging you with possession of a stolen vehicle…'

'What? I don't understand! No-one said it was stolen!'

'…and failure to report a death.'

'Are you serious?'

'Very. And I'm not finished yet. I'll add to the list in due course. Interview terminated at 8:41pm. Show Miss MacAllister to her room, would you, Constable.'

Munro smiled as he held the door open for West.

'Well done, lassie,' he said. 'Now, I suggest we get back to the Galloway and offer our apologies before they close the kitchen.'

Chapter 17

Unfortunately for Dougal, the much-anticipated fun-filled, firework display of an evening with Emily turned out to be nothing more than a brief encounter with a sparkler which fizzled out soon after he'd arrived. However, the fact that the female population of the UK apparently outnumbered the male – thereby increasing his chances of finding a suitable mate – provided him with a degree of comfort. But not as much comfort as a chocolate croissant dunked in a steaming mug of strong coffee.

Buoyed by the emails clogging his inbox, he consigned the previous night to history and was happily ploughing through them when West, looking suspiciously chipper, strolled through the door with Munro in tow.

'Dougal! You're in early,' she said. 'Aren't you tired?'

'Sorry?' said Dougal, miffed by the interruption.

'Last night? Late one, was it?'

'No, not particularly.'

'Really? I'd have thought, after a night of unbridled...'

'Charlie!' said Munro. 'Show some decorum. You're embarrassing the poor lad.'

'It's okay,' said Dougal, 'I'm used to it. By the by, it's all kicking off just now. Shall I fill you in while...'

'Oh, that can wait five minutes,' said West. 'I'll stick the kettle on and you can tell us about your date.'

'Do I have to?'

'Och, you'd best give her something, laddie,' said Munro, 'she'll be insufferable, otherwise.'

'There's not much to tell,' said Dougal. 'She was flat on her back by nine o'clock.'

'Come again?'

'Put it this way, the only thing she has in common with fish, is the way she drinks.'

'Oh dear,' said West, with a sympathetic tilt of the head, 'and there was I thinking you were off for a nice romantic meal for two.'

'You're not the only one,' said Dougal. 'Anyway, I'm not losing sleep over it, so can we move on?'

'Aye,' said Munro. 'Let's.'

'Okay. Jazz. Pathology's confirmed the cause of death as a cardiac arrest, they reckon it's an overdose but they're waiting on toxicology for confirmation.'

'Och, that's a given,' said Munro. 'Same as Buchanan. Meth. What else?'

Dougal reached into a brown paper sack sitting on his desk and produced a sealed plastic bag containing a single sheet of lined paper ripped from a notebook.

'Jazz's personal effects,' he said, 'they found this in his pocket.'

'What is it?' said West. 'Was he practising Sudoku?'

'It's a list of bank accounts, miss. No names, just sort codes and account numbers. One is the DNB in the Cayman Islands, the others are all in The Netherlands.'

'Bingo! So, that ties Jazz to Gundersen, right? It proves he was working for him after all.'

Munro glanced at West and shook his head.

'What?' she said. 'You're not convinced?'

'Not yet,' said Munro. 'Ask yourself the question, lassie, why would a taxi driver be carrying around such sensitive information on a scrap of paper in his jacket pocket?'

'Because someone gave it to him?'

'Why? Gundersen's accounts probably hold more cash than this country's gross GDP. He's not going to entrust that information to somebody driving a mini-cab. Go on, Dougal.'

'Interesting news from Brigadier Klassen. First of all, there's no sign of anything at the house in Oirschot...'

'Hardly surprising,' said West.

'...but he's also sent us the financial records from the Schemering Foundation. Get this – the proceeds from the sale of all the properties Rietveld acquired...'

'You mean Gundersen.'

'Two sides of the same coin, miss. Anyway, the proceeds went into the foundation's account. Okay? Simple enough. Then, no sooner had they cleared, almost every penny – bar a couple of thousand of quid – they went out again.'

'Doesnae take an Einstein to figure out where,' said Munro. 'Another company owned by Gundersen.'

'Correct. It's a supply agency. Nursing staff.'

'You're kidding?' said West as she doled out the tea. 'You mean that lowlife was actually employing people?'

'No, no,' said Dougal, 'that's just it. He didn't employ anyone, it was basically a shell company. On paper, all the money that went in to the agency account, went out in the guise of salaries, bonuses, general expenditure, etcetera. Basically, anything he could get away with.'

'Still an awful lot of dosh to set against comparatively paltry overheads, isn't it?'

'Not when the company's registered in the Cayman Islands, it isn't.'

'Hence the DNB account. Crafty bugger.'

'This Brigadier Klassen,' said Munro, 'is he not of a mind to close it down?'

'He has. Well, The Schemering Foundation, anyway. The supply agency's out of his jurisdiction.'

'Fair enough.'

'There's something else,' said Dougal. 'Klassen's tracked down four other personal bank accounts, two in the Netherlands and two in Norway. Nothing to do with those on the list, but they all received substantial payments from the supply agency and as soon as the transfers had cleared, the cash was taken out and the accounts closed.'

'So, why,' said West, 'have the Dutch not issued a European Arrest Warrant? I mean, I'd have thought they'd want to get their hands on him themselves.'

'They still might,' said Dougal, 'even though Gundersen's not a Dutch national, he still based the charity there and used it as a conduit to launder the cash, so there's every chance.'

'Works for me,' said West as she answered her phone. 'We find him, they extradite him, less paperwork. Perfect. Duncan, how's it going?'

'Miss. I thought you should know, I'm on Braemar Square. I've just had a quick look around the house Rietveld was renting, and it's empty.'

'Well, it would be, wouldn't it? He'd have cleared out as soon as…'

'No, no. I mean *empty*, as in, no-one's lived there for ages. There's no bed sheets, no clothes, no personal effects. Not even a smell of aftershave or shower gel.'

'Well, he must've been living there at some point, Duncan,' said West, 'why else would he rent it?'

'Who knows? Anyway, I'm told the landlord stays on the next street, I'm away to see him, just now. I'll give you a bell if I find anything.'

* * *

If there was one thing Duncan loathed about the public at large, it was the contempt they showed towards members of the police force when unexpectedly disturbed in the comfort of their own home during the course of an inquiry. However, whilst most had a propensity to howl, growl or scowl, or simply burst into tears, none had ever received him with the kind of welcome normally reserved for the bearer of a cheque from the National Lottery.

Belying his seventy-three years, the youthful Tam Paterson – with a shock of thick, white hair and a voice like a baritone – greeted him with open arms in a performance worthy of a department store Santa Claus intent on scaring the hell out of a four-year-old.

'Police!' he said, his voice booming across the street. 'You've come to tell me they've fixed my door, is that it?'

'Not exactly,' said Duncan, bewildered by the amateur dramatics, 'but they'll not be long, I'm sure.'

'Excellent! What can I do for you, Officer? You are an officer, aren't you?'

'I am. Detective Constable Reid, sir.'

'A detective! Can this day get any better?'

'I hope so,' said Duncan, stifling a grin. 'I just need to check, the house on Braemar Square, you are the landlord, right?'

'Landlord, owner and keeper of the faith. Indeed, I am.'

'And your name is?'

'Thomas! Call me Tam!'

'Okay. Can I have a wee word, Tam? About your tenant?'

'My tenant! Aye, of course! Come in, come in. Will you take a drink? I've not long boiled the kettle.'

'Aye,' said Duncan, smiling as he followed him inside. 'I will.'

* * *

Sitting within the confines of the kitchen, Paterson, eager to assist, lowered his voice to something approaching a normal level and handed Duncan a mug.

'So, tell me what you need to know, Detective, and I'll see if I can help. How's that?'

'That's perfect,' said Duncan, 'just perfect. Your tenant, Mr Rietveld, have you ever had any complaints about him, any trouble?'

'Not a peep,' said Paterson. 'He's the perfect gentleman – quiet, well-mannered. He's foreign, I think. Very well-to-do.'

'And have you any idea what he did for a living?'

'I've never asked. Probably works for a bank or something.'

'Probably?' said Duncan. 'Sorry, but do you not have to check your tenants' employment status before you take them on?'

'Not if I trust them.'

'What about the agency who look after the house, do they not want some assurance that the rent's going to be paid?'

'There is no agency,' said Paterson, sipping his tea. 'All they do is charge a high fee for changing a light bulb. I'll have none of that. It's a private let.'

'And he's always paid the rent on time? Never defaulted?'

'Never.'

'Cash or cheque?'

'Standing order. Every month, regular as clockwork.'

'And how did he get the house? What I mean is, how did you advertise it?'

'Shop window, up the way, there.'

'Okay. Now, you say it's a private let?'

'Aye, that's right.'

'Don't get me wrong, here, Tam,' said Duncan, 'I'm not trying to trip you up or anything, how you conduct your business is your affair, okay? I'm not interested in that. But was this a verbal arrangement you had with Mr Rietveld or did he sign a lease?'

'Why, he signed a lease, of course. I do everything by the book, Detective, it's all above board. Twelve months, renewable. Do you know where he's gone? I'll not find another like him.'

'I'm afraid not, we're still trying to locate him. Listen, would you happen to have a copy of the lease, here? Or do you keep it somewhere…'

'No, no. It's right here,' said Paterson as he reached across the table and opened the cutlery drawer, 'my filing system is second to none.'

Duncan took the manila envelope and pulled out a wodge of papers, frowning as he speed-read through them.

'Tam, I have to make a call,' he said as he gathered them up, 'do you mind if I take these with me? I'll be right back.'

* * *

Safe in the privacy of his car, Duncan spread out the sheets on the passenger seat and reached for his phone.

'Duncan, what's up? said West.

'Miss. Is Dougal with you? He needs to hear this.'

'Go ahead,' said West as she switched to speaker.

'Okay. I'm with the landlord of the house Rietveld was renting and it seems he's not as clever as we thought. I'm sending you a photo of the form that was sent to the bank to set up a standing order, it's got all his account details on it. It's the RBS on Sandgate.'

'Okay, we're on it,' said West, 'bit sloppy of him, considering.'

'Aye, schoolboy error, to say the least. But get this,' said Duncan, 'he took out the original lease nearly two years ago and the current one's up for renewal in a couple of months.'

'And?'

'His previous address is down as Kirkland Street, Maybole.'

'Okay, so what?'

'Kirkland Street,' said Dougal, leaping from his desk, 'is Alison Kennedy's address.'

'Well, that's alright isn't it?' said West, 'they obviously lived together at some point, then he moved out.'

'Miss,' said Dougal, incredulously, as he headed for the door, 'according to Alison Kennedy, she and Rietveld only met four months ago, Duncan's just told us the original lease is nearly two years old. She's been lying through her teeth.'

'At least someone's on the ball,' said West, flinching as the door slammed. 'Duncan, listen up, ask the landlord if you can take a look around the house. If Rietveld left in a hurry, chances are he may have forgotten something.'

'Roger that, miss. Thing is, we've not got a warrant.'

'Which is why you're going to ask him nicely, okay?'

* * *

Duncan, overshadowed by the gregarious Paterson, stood in the hollow lounge and, in the absence of any built-in cupboards, storage units or even a chimney breast, began unzipping the cushion covers on the two-seater sofa.

'I appreciate this, Tam, it's very good of you,' he said. 'I assume the furniture is yours, is that right?'

'Aye, it is,' said Paterson as he glanced around the room, bewildered. 'He's not much in the way of possessions, has he?'

'He's no possessions, full stop,' said Duncan. 'Have you not been here recently?'

'I only come when the lease is due for renewal, or unless there's a problem, so no. I've not been for almost a year.'

'Was it like this the last time you came?'

'No. I wouldn't say it was overflowing with bits and bobs, not by any stretch, but at least there were a few books about the place, coats hanging up, that sort of thing.'

'Okay. Let's try the kitchen,' said Duncan. 'I need you to stay with me, Tam. I may need a statement off you later just to verify I've not done anything untoward. Are you okay with that?'

'Perfectly.'

Had Duncan known what it was he was looking for, it may have incentivised him to search harder but, having checked the cupboards, the washing machine and the oven, all of which were bare, his enthusiasm was on the wane.

'This is incredible,' he said, despairingly, 'I mean, there's not even a tin of beans or a stale loaf of bread. He must've eaten everything before he left.'

'Will I look in here, for you?' said Paterson, pointing at the fridge, unsure if he was allowed to touch anything.

'Aye, may as well,' said Duncan. 'Check the freezer box as well.'

'Oh, it's as empty as a pauper's purse. It's been switched off, too.'

Duncan peered through the window at the overgrown garden.

'Is there anything out back, Tam?' he said. 'Do you have a tool shed, maybe?'

'No, just the weeds, by the looks of it.'

'A cellar?'

'Somewhere for my tenants to keep their fancy wine collection? I'm afraid not.'

'Upstairs?'

'Two bedrooms and the bathroom.'

'Okay, let's take a look, then that's us away.'

* * *

The bedrooms were identical. Same size, same wardrobes, same curtains, same divan beds, both stripped of linen, the mattress on one was still wrapped in its plastic shroud.

'It doesn't make any sense, Detective,' said Paterson as they moved to the bathroom. 'Why would the man be paying me rent if he's not staying here?'

'It's a mystery,' said Duncan, pointing to the bath panel. 'Would you mind if I had a peek behind here?'

'Be my guest. It should just pop off.'

Hoping to find something more than a couple of spiders and a handful of dust, Duncan eased it off and sighed.

'Well,' he said, perched on the edge of the tub, his arms resting on the wash basin. 'That's that. Thanks for your help, Tam, I appreciate it. You've saved us a lot of time, you know that?'

'Glad to be of service. Is there anything else I can help you with, before you go?'

'No, no,' said Duncan, pensively, as he toyed with the tap. 'You've done more than enough. Och, would you look at that, he's turned your water off, too.'

'Now, why on earth would he do that?'

'Beats me, but you'd best check the stopcock out front.'

'That'll not help,' said Paterson. 'The mains only runs to the kitchen. Everything else is fed from the tank.'

'The tank?'

'Aye. In the loft.'

* * *

Duncan, standing in the hallway, craned his neck and stared at the hatch in the ceiling.

'Can we get in there?' he said, removing his coat.

'Aye. There's a wee pole in the corner, there,' said Paterson, 'hook it into the latch and give it a tug, the ladder'll drop down.'

Duncan, torch in hand, moved gingerly up the steps and disappeared from view before reappearing moments later, head first, with a satisfied grin plastered across his face and water dripping down his arms.

'I've found out what's blocking your pipes,' he said as he passed down a small, plastic bag bound with gaffer tape. 'Would you place this on the floor for me, please.'

'What is it?'

'Evidence. There's more to come.'

Tam stacked all twelve packages neatly in a pile and stood to one side as Duncan slid down the ladder.

'What's in the bags, Detective?' he said, enthusiastically. 'Is it contraband? Or body parts, maybe?'

'Thankfully, no,' said Duncan, laughing. 'I'll let you know in due course, Tam, but unfortunately I'm afraid I'm going to have to ask you to leave now.'

'Oh,' said Paterson, dismayed. 'That is disappointing. Is it something I've done?'

'Aye. But in a good way, Tam. A very good way, indeed.'

* * *

West gathered up her notes, checked her watch and knocked back the last dregs of coffee as Munro relieved himself of his sling and flexed his shoulder.

'Are you sure you should be taking that off?' she said in a matronly manner.

'Never surer,' said Munro, 'my arm's been wasting away in that blessed thing. I'll have this stookie off tonight, as well.'

'Shouldn't a doctor do that?'

'I can handle a blade as well as the next man, lassie. Is that your phone?'

'Yes, it is. We're going to get you one today, then you can share the burden. Duncan, make it snappy, we're on our way out, Aletta's just arrived.'

'Oh, you need to hear this, miss. Trust me. You need to hear this.'

Chapter 18

According to the staff at the Glencree care home, Alison Kennedy – living up to her reputation as a selfless, earthbound angel – was purportedly meeting with Father Dalgetty to run through the eulogy for yet another dearly departed soul before returning home to enjoy what was left of her day off.

Torn between visiting St Cuthbert's and bestowing further grief upon the ageing priest, and concerned that what she'd told the care home may have been but a ruse to buy some time so she could abscond without fear of pursuit, Dougal – disappointed that someone as seemingly as honest as herself would lie about her relationship with Rietveld – gambled instead on visiting her at home.

Sitting astride his scooter, patience wearing thin, he reached for his phone.

'Duncan,' he said, checking his watch, 'are you all done there?'

'Aye, aye, Dougal. And guess what? You know that wee package you found up the chimney at Jazz's place?'

'Aye?'

'Well, I've found some more at the house Rietveld was renting. We now have a baker's dozen. Result, right?'

'Are you for real? That's brilliant,' said Dougal. 'Shame he's dead, it would've been nice to get a conviction.'

'I can't believe you said that. You, of all people. So, what's up?'

'Can you sort out a warrant for Kennedy's place and get yourself over here? Kirkland Street, by the school.'

'Roger that, pal. See you in ten.'

* * *

Dougal hopped into the passenger seat of the Audi, slumped back, and sighed.

'Something up?' said Duncan. 'Do you think there might be trouble? Is that why you called?'

'No, no,' said Dougal, 'there'll be no trouble. I just thought, if we're to bring her in, she's not going to jump on the back my scooter, is she? And this is more discreet than a squad car.'

'I wouldn't worry about being discreet; if her reputation's shot, it makes no difference what she travels in. So, where is she?'

'Gone to see the priest, then she's coming back here. Apparently. I just hope she's not done one. Listen, as we've got a minute, I think I owe you an apology. We didn't exactly get off on the right foot.'

'Nae bother. Forget it.'

'It's just that I never knew you'd worked with them before.'

'Them? You mean Westie and the chief? Oh, aye,' said Duncan. 'It was a hoot. They were up in Gourock. I was in uniform then. In fact, it was the chief who encouraged me to cross over to the dark side.'

'Is that so?'

'Right enough, and I've never looked back. Although, if I'm honest, I have to say, Dumfries isn't as dark as I'd like.'

'Either way,' said Dougal, 'no hard feelings? Okay?'

* * *

Duncan perked up as he noticed an attractive, bottle-blonde dressed in white jeans and an impossibly tight tee shirt, slinking her way along the street, jangling a set of door keys in one hand.

'That's not her, is it?' he said. 'I thought you said she was a fifty-something in charge of a care home?'

'She is.'

'If that's the case, pal, then that's the kind of place I'd like to end up in.'

* * *

Dougal stepped from the car and raised his arm in a half-hearted wave.

'Constable McCrae!' said Kennedy, as Duncan, hands in pockets, ambled up beside him. 'What a pleasant surprise, and I see you've brought a friend.'

'Aye, this is DC Reid, Miss Kennedy.'

'Alright?' said Duncan with a wink and a grin. 'Mind if we have a word. Inside?'

'My pleasure,' said Kennedy, coyly. 'Follow me.'

* * *

Duncan, not one to wait for an invitation, pulled up a chair as Kennedy tossed her keys on the table and sauntered towards the kitchen.

'So, what can I get you boys?' she said. 'Tea? Coffee?'

'Not for me, thanks,' said Dougal, hovering by the doorway.

'In that case,' said Kennedy, kicking off her shoes and curling up on the sofa, 'I'm going to relax. Father Dalgetty's a sweetie but he does take it out of you.'

'I'm sure he appreciates your help, Miss Kennedy,' said Dougal, 'can't be easy for someone of his age.'

'He's as strong as an ox, Constable. Just a bit slow, that's all. So, what can I do for you?'

Duncan locked eyes with Kennedy, took a deep breath and exhaled slowly.

'Just a few questions,' he said, grinning.

'It's about your ex,' said Dougal. 'Lucas Rietveld.'

'That bawbag?'

'Aye, I hope it's not too raw for you.'

'I can think of better things to talk about, but if we must. Come on, then. Let's have it.'

'Okay. You said you and Mr Rietveld first met four months ago, that's right, isn't it?'

'Aye,' said Kennedy, 'four months, or thereabouts, though God knows what I saw in the man. Hindsight, it's a wonderful thing, do you not think?'

'I do. If you don't mind me asking, did you ever live together? At the same address?'

'After four months? Hardly. Anyway, I'm not ready for that, not even at my age. He had his place, and I've got mine.'

'But he stopped over?'

'What do you think?'

'And did you ever stay at his?' said Dougal. 'Did you ever go to his house?'

'No. In fact, in all the time I knew him, I can safely say that I never went. Not even once.'

'Really?' said Duncan. 'And was that your choice?'

'Not exactly, but I wasn't complaining,' said Kennedy, purring. 'I like my own bed, Constable.'

'Who doesn't?'

Dougal, cringing at the flirtatious behaviour, stepped from the doorway and took a seat at the table.

'Have you always lived here, Miss Kennedy?' he said. 'I mean, this is your house, right?'

'Aye, it is. And I've paid off the mortgage, too.'

'Good for you. So, you've never lived anywhere else?'

'Apart from when I was a student, no.'

'And you've not been away for any length of time?'

'The longest I've been away is one week. About ten years ago. Tenerife. I'm not one for travelling.'

'Fair enough,' said Dougal, rubbing the side of his head.

'Are you okay, Constable?' said Kennedy. 'Have you a headache coming on?'

'It's not coming, Miss Kennedy. It's here. See, I've a wee problem with what you're telling us.'

'How so?'

'Well, when Lucas Rietveld rented that house on Braemar Square, he was asked to put down his previous address. And he did. This one.'

'Well, that's just typical of the bastard,' said Kennedy, huffing. 'Probably so's they'd come after me if he defaulted on the rent.'

'No,' said Duncan, dropping the cheeky grin, 'that's not it. See, Mr Rietveld took out a lease on that house nearly two years ago. That's nineteen months before you met. So, how does that work?'

Kennedy hesitated, stared first at Duncan, and then Dougal, before adopting a supercilious smile.

'Now what would I gain from lying to the police?' she said. 'Because if that's what you're implying, then perhaps I should call my lawyer.'

'I'd say that's an excellent idea,' said Dougal as he stood. 'Alison Kennedy, I'm arresting you on suspicion of interfering with an investigation and obstruction. You do not have to say anything but it may harm your defence if you do not mention when questioned, something you later rely on in court. Do you understand?'

Chapter 19

Although he'd never experienced the luxury of dining in a five-star hotel – the nearest he'd ever got was a three-star affair during a two-week break in Cumbria with his beloved Jean, and those had been painted on the wall by the owner himself – Munro, nonetheless, was an advocate of table manners. He sat with a napkin tucked firmly into his collar, carving up his pizza with a knife and fork like a mathematician with OCD whilst West, favouring what she considered to be the more authentic *continental* approach, used both hands to shovel it in like a ravenous squirrel in the first throes of winter.

'Heathen,' said Munro.

Dougal and Duncan tumbled through the door like a couple of errant schoolboys.

'Perfect timing,' said West, with a mouthful of margherita. 'Dive in.'

'Best be quick,' said Munro. 'Charlie's only had four slices and as you know, she's got the appetite of an abandoned bulldog on the backstreets of the Gorbals.'

Dougal helped himself and passed the box to Duncan.

'No toppings?' he said.

'Jimbo doesn't like pepperoni,' said West, 'or olives. Or pineapple. Or anchovies.'

'A pizza's no place for fruit, lassie. Let alone a hairy fish with a week's worth of salt in its gullet.'

West wiped her hands and slid a piece of paper across the desk.

'Before I forget,' she said, 'Jimbo's got a new mobile. Stick his number in, he'd love to hear from you.'

Duncan glanced across at Munro as he tapped the number into his phone.

'What's up with your arm, chief?' he said. 'Did you ditch the stookie?'

'Indeed, I did,' said Munro. 'Although, a word to the wise, should you ever have cause to remove one yourself, I'd think twice about using an angle grinder. It's not as easy as you think.'

'By the way,' said Dougal, 'Alison Kennedy's downstairs. We're holding her for obstruction. How'd you get on this morning? With Aletta?'

'Not a sausage,' said West, 'the poor woman doesn't know if she's coming or going. The last time she saw Jazz was when he left to do that airport run.'

'Or not. As the case may be. I still can't see why he'd want to lie about that. I mean, what was he hiding?'

Munro put down his cutlery, pulled the napkin from his collar, and moved to the kitchen.

'Perhaps,' he said, filling the kettle, 'he wasnae hiding anything at all.'

'Here we go,' said West. 'Jimbo's about to rock the boat, I can tell.'

'The footage from Kilbride's camera,' said Munro, 'it shows Jazz and MacAllister arriving at Carducci's place around mid-morning, is that not right, Duncan?'

'Aye, that's right, chief. About half ten, I think.'

'And according to Aletta, Jazz left the house around five-thirty, so that would've given him ample time to get to the airport and back before taking MacAllister over to Carducci's place.'

'Okay, I'll buy that,' said West. 'Go on.'

'We know Gundersen came back from Eindhoven on the three o'clock flight. Soon after he landed, he called Alison Kennedy to put an end to their relationship, then he telephoned Emily Fisher who, as we know, told him that the police had been snooping around. So, what if he decided to keep his head down and stop overnight in Edinburgh?'

'Genius!' said Dougal. 'That's why Jazz left at five-thirty. To pick up Gundersen!'

'Aye, okay,' said Duncan, 'that makes sense, but where did he take him? Not to his place on Braemar Square, that's for sure.'

Munro, sighing despondently at the ensuing silence, dropped a tea bag into each of the mugs, threw his head back, and closed his eyes for the count of ten.

'For the love of God!' he said, slamming the counter with the palm of his hand. 'Has no-one anything to say? By jiminy, surely you can work it out between the three of you?'

Dougal lowered his head in shame while West, frowning with the intensity of someone in need of a laxative, nibbled on her lower lip.

'Got it!' she said, confidently. 'Jazz didn't drop Gundersen anywhere! He was with him in the taxi the whole time.'

'Hallelujah!' said Munro, glowering at Dougal and Duncan. 'So, you two, monkey-see and monkey-do, what does that mean?'

'It means,' said Dougal, keeping his head down, 'that after they'd picked up MacAllister, he had the perfect opportunity to take care of Jazz and then return the car to the yard at Kestrel.'

'No, hold on,' said West, standing to relieve Munro of his kitchen duties, 'that doesn't work. They'd have had to ask Beth for the key and she would've told us that.'

'Not if they didn't need one,' said Duncan. 'Jazz didn't have any keys on him when I searched his pockets. Stands to reason, Gundersen must've lifted them.'

Munro returned to his seat, folded his arms and stared across the desk.

'So,' he said, 'fingers on buzzers. Final question. Why? Why would Gundersen want to murder Jazz Banerjee?'

'Because,' said Dougal, wary of sticking his head above the parapet, 'he'd been crossed? Jazz had a bundle of meth stuffed up his chimney, right? So, maybe he was trying to peddle the stuff himself and got found out.'

'Aye. It's possible,' said Munro. 'But do you not think the death penalty's a wee bit harsh for a simple case of theft?'

'Maybe not,' said Dougal, 'considering he had a note of Gundersen's accounts on him, maybe it wasn't just the fact that he had the drugs, maybe he was accessing his accounts and depleting his funds?'

'Makes sense to me,' said West.

'Not to me, it doesn't, Charlie!' said Munro, raising his voice. 'Not by a long chalk. How did he get hold of those account numbers? Why did he do it? What's the link? Where's the motif?'

Munro went the window and stood, hands clasped behind his back.

'Dear God! Can you lot not think for yourselves? Look, who did Gundersen meet in Oslo, way back when?'

'Angus Buchanan and Remo Carducci,' said Dougal.

'Good. And after using them to expand his business, what did they do?'

'They forced him out.'

'Good. Anita Carducci goes inside giving Lars Gundersen…?

'The ideal opportunity to muscle in on the business?'

'At last. We're getting somewhere.'

'So,' said West, demolishing the last slice of cold pizza, 'Anita Carducci gets out, tries to pick up where she and Remo left off, and ends up with her throat slit because Gunderen's trying to reclaim what he sees as rightfully his.'

'Hold on,' said Dougal, 'if that's the case, then maybe the gear we found up the chimney didn't belong to Gundersen at all. Maybe it belonged to Anita Carducci.'

'Makes no odds who it belonged to,' said West. 'Either way, the fact that he had it is reason enough to want him out of the way.'

'And what about the account details?' said Munro. 'Where did they come from?'

'Well,' said Dougal, 'if we assume MacAllister's not being entirely truthful about knowing her passenger in the Golf, then she'd be the obvious source. And she knows Jazz, so she could easily have given them to him.'

'No,' said West as she began pacing the room, wagging her finger in the air, 'that doesn't add up. MacAllister's too lightweight for that, but, she got pally enough with Carducci to move in with her, right? So, what if MacAllister gave the account details to Carducci so that, between them, they could ruin Gundersen.'

'Then why pass them on to Jazz?' said Munro, relieved, at last, that they were making some headway.

'Easy. Carducci's done time and MacAllister's on a suspended sentence. One foot wrong and they'd both be back inside, whereas Jazz has no previous and, if their intention was to plunder the accounts, then he's got a legit business they could use to launder the cash.'

'Well,' said Munro, 'it's a theory, at least. Which is more than we had ten minutes ago. Okay, Duncan, I need you to call every hotel in Edinburgh, start with those in the vicinity of the airport, and see if Gundersen checked in under either name.'

'Roger that, chief.'

'And before you do that, call Beth at the taxi office. See if she had any contact with Jazz, any contact at all, before he went off-air.'

Duncan pulled his phone from his pocket and read a single text.

'Dougal,' he said, 'you're good to go, pal. Warrant's come through.'

'Warrant?' said West. 'For where?'

'Kennedy's place,' said Dougal. 'I'm going for a snoop around.'

'Okay, cool. Be as quick as you can. We'll interview her just as soon as you're back.'

'I almost forgot,' said Duncan, tossing a pile of envelopes on the desk as Dougal fled the room. 'I must've picked these up by mistake.'

'What are they?' said West, dragging them towards her.

'Bank statements, mainly. And a couple of mobile phone bills.'

'Hold on, these belong to Alison Kennedy. Are you telling me you took these from…? Duncan, for Christ's sake, do you know…?'

'Well, laddie,' said Munro, grinning, 'I do believe you're on the road to redemption. Now, you'd best get on the phone while I attempt to erase those envelopes from my memory.'

* * *

West put the phone bills to one side, ripped open the bank statements and, having arranged them in chronological order, sat with her head in her hands, analysing the figures in the credit column.

'Doing alright for someone in her position,' she said, placing a tick next to some figures while marking others with a yellow highlighter. 'Jimbo, take a look at this. The ones with a tick are obviously her salary – Glencree

Limited, same amount, every month. Now, look at the ones in yellow.'

Munro took his glasses from his breast pocket, perched them on the end of his nose, and drew a breath as he perused the figures.

'My, my,' he said, with a subtle shake of the head. 'There's no doubt it. The woman has a healthy sideline in something. Twelve thousand pounds?'

'That's just this month,' said West, 'look at the others. Seventeen last month.

'And twenty-two the month before. I wonder if she's looking for a business partner.'

'Pass me that bit of paper from Jazz's stuff, would you?'

West compared the list of foreign account numbers to those on Kennedy's statement, looked at Munro and smiled.

'Cayman,' she said. 'All those massive sums came from the same account in the Cayman Islands…'

'I bet she's not declared it on her tax return.'

'…so, the question is…'

'The question is, Charlie, why would the man she knows as Rietveld transfer so much money into the account of a lowly, care home worker?'

West stared unblinkingly at Munro as though the answer would come to her via the gift of telepathy.

'Because,' she said, smirking, 'that was her fee. Her slice of the proceeds from the sale of the properties he'd pilfered from the people in the home. She was tipping him off, giving him the inside track on who was about to pop their clogs, and that's when he swooped in and drafted their wills.'

'Chief!' said Duncan, yelling from across the room, 'I just spoke with Beth from the taxi office. She said she did speak to Jazz, just after midday, apparently.'

'And?'

'He wasn't very talkative. She says she only called to ask if he was available for a couple of jobs and he fair took her head off. He said he'd just been to Glebe Crescent and was en route to another pick-up.'

'Is that it?'

'No,' said Duncan, grinning, 'guess where he was going? Glencree.'

Munro removed his glasses and rubbed his eyes.

'Well,' he said, wearily, 'it would appear Miss MacAllister was telling the truth after all. Jazz did drop her off. At Robbie's place.'

'Aye,' said Duncan, 'and then he went to Glencree to pick up Alison Kennedy.'

Chapter 20

Despite the position offering successful applicants similar benefits to an all-inclusive holiday resort – including free meals and accommodation – the majority of candidates invited to attend an interview would invariably adopt an aggressive and understandably defensive attitude when fielding questions from the panel, batting them back with obtuse, sometimes facetious, but more often than not, less than candid answers, in an attempt to avoid incriminating themselves.

Alison Kennedy, however – having spent decades dealing with not only the sick and the dying, but their grief-stricken relatives as well – was a past-master at keeping calm in the face of adversity. Unfazed by her surroundings, she sat, as cool as a cucumber, waiting for her hosts to arrive.

'Ah, Constable McCrae,' she said, greeting him with a smile, 'have you not brought your dashing friend with you?'

'No, no, Miss Kennedy. I've two others I'd like you to meet. DS West, and this is Detective Inspector Munro.'

'Inspector?' said Kennedy. 'I do so like a man with some experience under his belt.'

'Is that so?' said Munro, taking a seat.

'Indeed. I find they're much more open to reason. There's an air of logic to their way of thinking and they're not given to making rash, impulsive decisions based purely on circumstance.'

'You're probably right.'

'And,' said Kennedy, with the subtlest of winks, 'they know a good thing when they see it.'

Munro – the crow's feet around his piercing, blue eyes accentuated by his almost bashful smile – leaned forward and hesitated before he spoke.

'You know something, Miss Kennedy?' he said, softly. 'If I was ten years younger…'

'Yes, Inspector?'

'…I'd have thrown the book at you by now. But, as I've mellowed with age, I'm going to drag this out a wee bit longer. It's so much more enjoyable that way.'

West, trying to keep her mouth from curling at both ends, cleared her throat and stabbed the voice recorder.

'DS West,' she said. 'Also present, DC McCrae, DI Munro and Miss Alison Kennedy. Shall we begin?'

Kennedy folded her arms and forced a smile.

'After you, Sergeant.'

'Okey dokey. Lucas Rietveld. Your boyfriend. Your ex-boyfriend. You met a few months ago, is that right?'

'About four months ago, aye, that's right.' said Kennedy. 'Give or take a few weeks.'

'Excellent,' said West. 'And you've never lived together? Co-habited? Shared the same address?'

'No. We have not.'

'But he visited you a lot? At your house? On Kirkland Street?'

'He did.'

'How often would you say that was? Twice a week? Three times? Four?'

'He'd stay most weekends,' said Kennedy. 'And he'd come by once or twice during the week. Depending on his schedule.'

'So, when he visited you, Miss Kennedy,' said Dougal, 'did he visit with the intention of stopping over, or was that a more impulsive decision?'

'I don't see why that would make a difference,' said Kennedy.

'Well, I'm just wondering if would bring an overnight bag, that's all.'

'He did, aye. Most of the time.'

'Okay, so, he had no need for all those clothes in your wardrobe?'

'I'm not sure I follow.'

'Your wardrobe,' said Dougal, 'it's half full of men's clothes. As is your laundry basket, and there are a couple of gentleman's overcoats hanging in the closet in the hallway.'

'Do you know,' said Kennedy, feigning surprise, 'I've never noticed. They must've just accumulated over time.'

'Aye, that must be it. And just out of interest, do you have a favourite perfume, or do you tend to chop and change, as the mood suits?'

'I only wear Cacherel, Constable. Always have done. Is this going somewhere?'

'I hope so. What I mean is, you're not a fan of Calvin Klein, then, are you?'

'No.'

'CK One?'

'No.'

'Aftershave?'

Kennedy bowed her head and coughed politely into her hand as Munro, deliberately avoiding any eye contact, stood up, crossed his hands behind his back, and walked slowly around the room.

'You're the manager of the Glencree care home, that's right, isn't it?' he said, quietly.

'I am, indeed.'

'And do you enjoy your work?'

'It's very rewarding.'

'Och, I'm sure it is,' said Munro. 'In more ways than one. It's a commendable thing you do. Akin to nursing, in a way.'

'Thank you.'

'And the pay's okay, is it? I mean, unlike the nurses, you're not struggling to make ends meet?'

'The pay is more than adequate. And no, I'm not struggling.'

Munro, stopped six feet behind her chair, and paused momentarily.

'Tell me,' he said, 'do you have much disposable income, Miss Kennedy?'

'I think you'll find that's my business, Inspector.'

'Aye, you're quite right,' said Munro. 'It was rude of me to ask. Only, I was just wondering, here you are – young, free and single, with a good job and no mortgage. You dinnae strike me as someone who squanders their money.'

'I save what I can, if that's what you're driving at.'

'So, you've not cashed-in any investments recently? A private pension, maybe, or some stocks and shares? A premium bond, perhaps?'

'I have not, no.'

'Then perhaps you can explain the fifty-one thousand pounds that appeared in your bank account over the last three months?'

Kennedy, without so much as a blink, turned to Munro and smiled.

'Must be a bank error,' she said. 'I wish I'd noticed, I'd have spent it.'

West, warming to Kennedy's ice-cold performance, sat back and folded her arms.

'How well do you know Jasminder Banerjee?' she said.

'Who?'

'Jazz.'

'I've met him once. I think. When he picked me up from Glencree.'

'And you got on well?'

'We talked. A little.' said Kennedy. 'I tend not to fraternise with taxi drivers.'

'Okay. What about Anita Carducci?'

'Sorry. I don't know anyone called Anita.'

'Oh, you must do, surely,' said West. 'She owned a chain of restaurants with her husband, Remo. Very successful they were, too. And, they had a very lucrative sideline running a... a pharmacy business.'

'What's that got to do with me?'

'They had to close,' said Munro.

'Shame,' said Kennedy. 'Debt, was it? Did they get in over their heads?'

'Not exactly, no. Let's just say, a death in the family forced them into early retirement.'

'Let's try another,' said West, as Munro returned to his seat. 'Let's see if this one rings any bells. Lars Gundersen.'

Kennedy crossed her legs, glanced at Dougal and smiled as if butter wouldn't melt.

'Can I go soon, Constable?' she said, only to be interrupted by a brief knock on the door, whereupon Duncan stepped into the room, slid a folded piece of A4 across the table, and promptly left.

West gave it a cursory glance before flashing it under Dougal's nose and passing it to Munro who placed it face down on the desk.

'Tell me, Miss Kennedy,' he said, clasping his hands beneath his chin, 'how do you travel to work?'

'Public transport. Or taxi.'

'A taxi. Of course. Do you not drive, yourself?

'Not anymore,' said Kennedy. 'I gave it up, I simply don't have the need.'

'I see. And was that relatively recently?'

'Relatively. Aye.'

'You know, I have a theory about motor cars,' said Munro, 'I believe they reflect the personality of the owner. Take mine, for example, it's an old Peugeot estate. It's almost knackered, has a few rust spots here and there, but apart from the occasional, unexpected blow-out from the exhaust, it's steadfast. Reliable.'

'That's very interesting, Inspector,' said Kennedy.

'Whereas you, I imagine, you'd drive something a wee bit sportier. Something like a hatchback, perhaps?'

'Well, I've got to hand it to you,' said Kennedy, 'you're on the money, there.'

'I thought so. I'll go one better. I'd even wager it was white.'

'Indeed it was. How perceptive of you.'

'Not really, Miss Kennedy. It's really quite obvious to me. You see, I suit black, it reflects my moods. But you suit white. There's something quite innocent about white, don't you think? Like a wedding dress. For the benefit of the tape, I am showing Miss Kennedy a copy of a marriage certificate obtained from the National Registry of Norway. The certificate shows that a Mr Lars Gundersen, occupation: chemist, was married to a Miss Alison Kennedy, occupation: student, in a civil ceremony at the County Court, Oslo.'

Kennedy, completely unflustered, took a deep breath and offered the same patronising smile she gave to those who neither knew, nor cared, about her.

'Being married's not a crime, Inspector,' she said.

'You're quite right, of course,' said Munro. 'It isn't. But murder is. See here, Miss Kennedy, apart from all the evidence we have that connects you to Lars Gundersen, also known as Lucas Rietveld, we also have some strands of hair. Human hair we took from the boot of a car. A boot containing the body of Jasminder Banerjee.'

'Do convey my condolences,' said Kennedy.

'The hair was snarled around a tow-rope that was used to tie him up.'

'Is that so?'

'Aye, it is. But what excites me about these strands of hair, is that they're not in their natural state. They've been bleached, bleached to a shade much like your own.'

'The wonders of hydrogen peroxide.'

'Exactly. The bottom line, Miss Kennedy, is once we're done here, we're going to take a wee swab from you for DNA profiling. Now, I'm not a betting man, myself, but I'd lay a year's salary on us getting a perfect match between the two…'

'Gambling. Bad habit, Inspector. Much wiser to invest it.'

'…which would then place you at the scene, making you an accessory, at the very least.'

'I'll protest my innocence, of course,' said Kennedy. 'I'm sure I've an alibi lying around somewhere.'

'We'll need a sample of your handwriting, too,' said Dougal, holding up the plastic bag containing the list of account numbers, 'to get a match to these.'

'Oh, there's no need to waste your time doing that,' said Kennedy. 'You'll find the notebook that page came from on the dining table.'

'So, you admit to writing these down?'

'Don't look so surprised.'

'And you know who they belong to?'

Kennedy raised her eyebrows and smiled.

'Why did you give them to Jazz?' said West.

'Second choice,' said Kennedy. 'I had planned to pass them on to Father Dalgetty but he's got a few years left in him, yet.'

'So, hold on, you meet Jazz for the first time, give him some bank details, and he doesn't question it?'

'He didn't know. What I gave Jazz was a sealed envelope, Sergeant. He thought it was a cheque against the Glencree account.'

'Why?'

'Because I knew he'd put it straight in his pocket and, sooner or later, you'd find it.'

'What made you so sure?' said West. 'I mean, how did you know we'd find it?'

'I'd heard a rumour,' said Kennedy, 'about his... heart condition.'

Munro fixed Kennedy with a steely gaze.

'What was the purpose of all this?' he said, frowning with intrigue.

Kennedy glanced ruefully at the ceiling and shook her head.

'I had to teach him a lesson,' she said. 'I don't like being made a fool of, Inspector.'

'Teach who a lesson? Your husband? Gundersen?'

'He was spending a lot of time away from home.'

Munro sat back and regarded Kennedy with a curious tilt of the head.

'I have to say, for as long as we've been aware of your husband's activities, Miss Kennedy, that would appear to be par for the course. So, why the concern?'

'I may not be as pure as the driven snow, Inspector, but I have my faith, and if there's one thing I do believe in, it's fidelity.'

'Go on,' said West, her interest heightened as the questioning turned to gossip. 'Are you saying he was having an affair?'

Kennedy dropped the smile and stared at West, her face suddenly cold and hard.

'Probably not the first,' she said, 'and almost certainly not the last.'

'So, this was your revenge?'

'Not a word I'm fond of, Sergeant. I care to think of it as... retribution.'

'And this had been going on for a while then, had it? This affair?'

'A year or two,' said Kennedy. 'I kept telling myself I was being paranoid but, you know how it is, I had to prove to myself that I was wrong. So, one day I followed him, and he led me all the way to Prestwick.'

'Prestwick? So, you know who she is then?'

'Indeed, I do,' said Kennedy. 'Does the name Clare MacAllister mean anything to you?'

'Not really,' said West, pursing her lips.

'Well, if you're wondering where my husband is, I suggest you make her your first port of call.'

'Thanks for the tip.'

Munro placed the marriage certificate in his breast pocket and hauled himself to his feet.

'Before I go, Miss Kennedy,' he said, heading for the door. 'Jazz Banerjee. Why did your husband kill Jazz Banerjee?'

'Oh, you'll have to ask him that yourself, Inspector. When you find him.'

Chapter 21

Duncan, his rarely-ruffled air of insouciance shattered by a sudden bout of anxiety, paced around the office like an expectant father banished from the delivery room as he waited nervously for the others to return.

'So?' he said, excitedly, as they traipsed through the door. 'What's the verdict? Is she guilty, or what?'

'Of murder?' said Munro, pulling up a chair. 'No. She's not guilty of murder. But she is guilty of being an accessory, if not an accomplice.'

'Result!' said Duncan, clapping his hands. 'So, are we not going to do her for her involvement in the property scam, as well? I mean, there must be a half a dozen charges we can lay at her feet.'

'All in good time,' said West, 'there's plenty more coming her way, don't you worry. For starters, those account numbers? It was Kennedy who gave them to Jazz.'

'Kennedy?' said Duncan, looking startled. 'I'm confused. I mean, why?'

'To get back at Gundersen, of course. She wanted to hit him where it hurts.'

'No, no. I mean, why Jazz?'

'Well, for one, she knew that sooner or later, we'd find the list and figure out the link to Gundersen. And two, with Jazz brown bread, Gundersen wouldn't be able to link them back to her.'

'All that, just because he'd phoned her from the airport and dumped her?'

'He did no such thing, laddie,' said Munro, his mind drifting. 'That was just a smokescreen for our benefit. You're forgetting, they're husband and wife. She did it because Gundersen and Clare MacAllister were at it hammer and tongs behind her back.'

'Gundersen and MacAllister? Are you joking me? So, hold on a minute, that means when Gundersen went to the hospital to send you on your way to the happy ever after, it wasn't Jazz who'd asked MacAllister to take him there, he probably just asked her, himself?'

'Aye, more than likely.'

Having somewhat masochistically saddled himself with the task of seeking out a logical rationale for Kennedy's actions, Duncan – experiencing the kind of mental anguish not seen since his first, and only, attempt at the Times crossword – scratched the back of his head as he continued to wear out the floor.

'Okay,' he said, 'am I missing something here? See, if Kennedy gave those numbers to Jazz, then that would've been in the last day or two, right?'

'Indeed, it would,' said Munro.

'But she'd already come to us about Dalgetty's pal, about the irregularities with the will. So, she must've known she'd be running the risk of getting caught, surely?'

'Of course, she did,' said West, 'but she probably thought that with no previous and a good brief, even if she was charged with something, she'd get off lightly.'

'More fool her.'

'Yup, but if she was going to go through with her plan to bring about Gundersen's downfall, then she had to risk it. The fact that she'd already told us about Margaret

Forsyth actually worked in her favour. She was playing carrot to our donkey.'

'Was that not just a wee bit dangerous?' said Duncan. 'I mean, Gundersen's still out there, he'll be raging.'

'That, he will,' said Munro. 'No doubt about it.'

Duncan hoisted himself onto a table and sat with his hands tucked beneath his legs.

'Well, fair play to the lassie,' he said, resignedly, 'but I wouldn't like to be in her shoes just now. It seems like an awful lot of effort to go to if all she wanted was for us to track him down and put him away.'

'Aye, and that's easier said than done,' said Munro, rapping the desk with his fingers, 'we've not had any luck so far and nothing's going to change just because some lassie comes up with a hair-brained scheme to kick him in the assets, I can tell you.'

'So, I take it we're still none the wiser? We've still no idea where he is?'

'Nope,' said West, smiling, 'we haven't a clue. And at this precise moment in time, I don't care, either.'

'See here, Charlie!' said Munro, slamming the desk as his frustration boiled over. 'That's precisely the kind of attitude that'll keep those three stripes on your shoulder! I do care. The man's a menace and frankly, if he can go away and reinvent himself as Lucas Rietveld, then God knows what he'll do next, but I'll tell you this for nothing, I'll not rest until I've found him. Him and the rest of his kind. Have you got that?'

'Loud and clear,' said West, reaching for her coat. 'And on that cheery note, I suggest we all go down the pub and drown our sorrows. Especially Jimbo's. First round's on me.'

'Not for me, thanks, miss,' said Dougal. 'I'm scootering.'

'Okay. Duncan?'

'Aye, I could murder a pint, but I'm away back to Dumfries.'

'Good, you can give me a lift,' said Munro. 'I've no faith in taxi drivers, just now.'

'What do you mean?' said West, 'I thought you were crashing at mine until we'd sorted this out?'

'Nothing personal, Charlie, but I need some time to think, to see if I cannae figure out what Gundersen's up to next. A night in front of the telly will do you no harm. Give your brain a rest.'

'Yeah, right. Nothing like being on your own with a flask of Chianti and some cheese on toast.'

'Not necessarily,' said Munro. 'Dougal, are you giving that wee lassie of yours a second spin of the wheel, tonight?'

'No chance. Not unless she's given up alcohol.'

'Good. In that case, would you mind stopping with Charlie? It's not a good idea for either of you to be alone while the Viking's still at large.'

'Aye, no bother. Miss, is that okay with you?'

'Certainly is, Dougal,' said West, chirpily. 'And I'll tell you what, as Jimbo's not joining us, I'm going to treat you to an Indian.'

'Right,' said Munro, as he and Duncan turned for the door. 'That's us away then. We'll talk tomorrow.'

'Not so fast,' said West, 'have you got your phone with you?'

'I have.'

'Then text me. Let me know you're home safe.'

'Home safe? Good grief, lassie, you're worse than Jean ever was.'

Chapter 22

Not one for table etiquette when hunger prevailed, West, dispensing with the formalities, handed Dougal a plate, opened all the foil containers and drove her fist through a mountain of poppadoms.

'Here you go,' she said, 'a tikka masala for you, and a scorching vindaloo for me.'

'I don't how you can eat that, it must rot your insides.'

'Nonsense! All that chilli, it's good for you. Keeps the circulation going.'

'Aye, and that's not the only thing,' said Dougal, raising his glass of orange juice. 'Cheers. Did you lock the door?'

'Sure did,' said West, swigging her beer, 'there's no way the big, bad wolf's getting in here tonight, so you can relax.'

Dougal, forsaking the boiled rice for something less exotic but infinitely more palatable, spooned his entire portion of curry over a plateful of chips and stirred vigorously.

'I thought I might go see Father Dalgetty tomorrow,' he said. 'You know, pay him a courtesy call and fill him in on what's happened.'

'Good idea,' said West. 'I'm not sure it'll put his mind at rest, though. In fact, it'll probably shatter his faith in human nature.'

'Aye, right enough. But best he knows. I still can't get over it, myself. Alison Kennedy, eh? Who'd have thought?'

'Two words,' said West. 'Book. Cover. Although, the same could be said for Clare MacAllister. Never thought I'd see the day when she started telling the truth.'

'Not exactly innocent, though, is she?'

'Not exactly, no, but…'

West put down her fork, took another swig of beer and stared quizzically into space.

'You okay?' said Dougal.

'When we went to pick her up, from Robbie's place…'

'Aye?'

'…he got quite aggressive, wouldn't let us in. He was adamant MacAllister wasn't there, until we read him the riot act. Why? Why was he trying to protect her?'

'Maybe he knows something?'

'Maybe. Why else would he be so defensive?'

'Could it be,' said Dougal, 'that he and Jazz were in it together? You know, the wee package wedged up the chimney?'

'Do we know what his day job is? Apart from helping out at Kestrel?'

'Something to do with the NHS, I think.'

'You're kidding, right? What, a doctor or something?'

'No, no,' said Dougal. 'Office work, I think. Admin or something.'

'Really?'

'I'll to have check but, aye. Why?'

'I'm suddenly thinking about those tablets. Do we know what they are yet?'

'No. Are you thinking…?'

'If they're prescription drugs, and he's in a position to get them, then who knows? There's only one way to find out. Let's bring him in, have a word. As soon as you're back from seeing Dalgetty.'

'Aye, okay.'

West, returning to the task at hand, tore off a large chunk of naan bread, dipped it in the curry sauce and stuffed it in her mouth as she checked her phone.

'Still no word,' she said, 'from Jimbo, I mean.'

'It's too soon,' said Dougal. 'Even if Duncan went hell for leather, they'd still not be back yet. Give it half an hour, then another for him to get settled.'

'Yeah, you're right. I worry too much.'

'Is he okay, do you think? I mean, he fair lost the plot when he was raging about Gundersen, and he didn't hold back when he ripped into us.'

'Wouldn't worry about it, Dougal,' said West with a smile. 'He's old school. A tongue-lashing's just his way of bringing out the best in you.'

'I can think of less abrasive methods,' said Dougal. 'That Gundersen, he's got under his skin, hasn't he?'

'Yup, he's certainly rattled his cage, that's for sure, and if I know Jimbo, he means what he says. He's not going to stop until he's banged up for good.'

* * *

According to the saying, the best part of going away is the coming home – an adage to which Munro would have readily subscribed were it not for the distant honking of the Canada geese, the occasional shriek of a barn owl, the sound of the waves crashing onto the shore, and the fact that he'd forgotten to buy a fresh pint of milk.

He peered through the windscreen at the row of lifeless cottages, concluded that his neighbours were either on their holidays or getting blootered in the pub, and checked his watch.

'Well,' said Duncan, 'that has to be one of the quietest journeys I've ever made. Are you okay, chief? You've not said a word since we passed Carronbridge.'

Munro, looking as though he'd been roused from a nap, turned to face him.

'Aye,' he said, a look of mild bewilderment on his face. 'Sorry, laddie, my mind's elsewhere. Thanks for the lift. I appreciate it.'

'Nae bother, chief. Always a pleasure. Will I come in?'

'Not on a first date.'

'No, no,' said Duncan, laughing, 'I wasn't after a coffee, I just meant, to check…'

'Aye, I know what you meant, but you're alright. I have things to do. Supper being one of them. You take yourself off and I'll see you on the morrow.'

* * *

With Duncan safely out of sight, Munro – adopting a sense of urgency not seen since his hasty, and somewhat premature, departure from the hospital – hurried inside and headed straight for the kitchen. Phone in hand, he turned the oven up full, took a pie from the fridge and placed it on the counter alongside a tin of baked beans and a bottle of brown sauce.

Checking his watch for a second time, he stepped to the lounge, hung his coat on the back of a chair and drew the curtains before pouring himself a large Balvenie and sitting at the dining table where, shrouded in the partial gloom with the theme to The Big Country playing softly in the background, he waited patiently for his visitor to arrive.

* * *

'You took your time,' he said, casually raising his glass. 'I've had you in the wing mirror for the last forty minutes.'

Dressed in a dark, blue suit and looking even taller in the flesh than he did on CCTV, Lars Gundersen, hands in pockets, stood, stern-faced, by the door.

'Will you take a drink?'

'Why not?' said Gundersen. 'I feel like celebrating.'

'You should tell your face. It's not exactly in a party mood.'

Gundersen took two steps forward and reached for the glass.

'Skål,' he said, knocking it back. 'You look well, Munro. Considering your injuries. Are you in pain?'

'No, no. Me and pain were separated at birth.'

'That soon? Then you've missed out on one of life's greatest pleasures.'

'I'm not sure about that,' said Munro, pointing at the bottle. 'Will you take another?'

Gundersen, his sharp features accentuated by the dim glow of the standard lamp, shook his head.

'Well, you'll not mind if I do. It's been quite a day.'

'Don't worry. It will be over soon.'

'Och, I've no doubt about that,' said Munro with a smirk, 'no doubt at all. So, come on, then, let's have it. There's more to this than Buchanan and Carducci, isn't there?'

Gundersen, toying with his empty glass, paused before answering.

'It's not nice when you're pushed out of business,' he said, 'when people you employ to help expand your interests and share in your success, get greedy and force you to one side. It's bullying. Just like school.'

'Oh, I wouldnae know about that,' said Munro, smiling as he swirled his malt, 'see, I was incredibly popular at school. Everybody wanted to be my pal. But you, I bet you were walloped as a wean.'

'Jealousy,' said Gundersen, tersely, 'often manifests itself as contempt.'

'Is that a fact? Tell me then, who was more jealous, was it Jazz? Or was it you?'

'You're talking in riddles.'

'Oh, it's quite simple,' said Munro, 'let me explain. See, if Jazz was jealous, jealous of your *success*, then that would explain why he stole some of your gear to sell on himself. But, if it was yourself who was bitten by the green-eyed monster, then that could only be because Jazz was seeing Clare MacAllister behind your back.'

Gundersen's top lip twitched as if afflicted by a tic.

'You're playing games, Munro,' he said, sniffing the empty glass. 'What makes you think Clare was seeing a common taxi driver?'

'Oh, the fact that he was wearing her lipstick, for a start. The thing is, Gundersen, you went after the wrong person. See, you should've gone after MacAllister, she has a history of philandering. In fact, she's perfected the art of making men go weak at the knees before taking what she wants and tossing them aside.'

Munro, relishing the sight of Gundersen racked with a burning resentment, continued to fuel his rage with the kind of jibes designed to dent the alpha-male ego.

'Just for the record,' he said, sipping his whisky, 'and I speak with experience of others who have trodden the well-worn path to her door, you might like to know that you are not the kindest man she's ever met. Nor are you the most intelligent man she's ever met. And, without wanting to get too personal, I can almost guarantee you're not the best lover she's ever had. I'm afraid you and Jazz, the pair of you dunderheids, are just the latest on her long list of losers.'

'Perhaps I will have that drink after all,' said Gundersen, reaching for the bottle.

'I imagine it probably makes you feel quite inadequate,' said Munro. 'Aye, that's the word. Inadequate.'

'You're pushing your luck, Munro.'

'Oh, I've not even started yet, trust me. I cannae wait to tell Alison.'

'Alison?'

'Aye. The woman you've betrayed. Your wife. Remember her? You can drop the charade, Gundersen, we know the two of you are married and she's currently in it up to her neck.'

'Where is she?'

'Probably having a wee lie down in her cell, about now.'

'You've arrested her?'

'Oh aye,' said Munro. 'She's a very pleasant lady, is Alison. And you know what I like about her? She enjoys a wee natter. She's told us quite a few interesting facts about the Cayman Islands. And Esme Sinclair. And Margaret Forsyth.'

'Is that so?' said Gundersen, his heckles raised.

'Aye, it is. I'm curious, though. See, Margaret Forsyth, she wasnae living at Glencree. So, how did you meet her? It couldnae be through Alison.'

Gundersen glanced at Munro and smirked.

'The priest introduced us,' he said. 'Father Dalgetty.'

'Really? And how did you two meet? It wasnae in the confessional, now, was it?'

'It was a fund-raising event. At Glencree.'

'Of course it was,' said Munro. 'The same fund-raising event where you and Alison Kennedy met for the first time. Apparently.'

Gundersen took a large gulp of whisky and turned towards the kitchen.

'You must be hungry,' he said, leaning in the doorway. 'I've interrupted your dinner.'

'Nae bother. I've not got the appetite just now.'

Munro, folded his arms, rested his hand on his chin, and stared at Gundersen in the same way one might regard an over-sized canvas hanging in an art museum.

'You're a clever man,' he said, dryly.

'Very.'

'Modest, too. I'll give you that. So, tell me, why would an intelligent chap like yourself want to get his hands dirty, again? I mean, juggling meth in the seedy world of users and pushers? Is that not a wee bit below yourself these days?'

'I don't get my hands dirty,' said Gundersen. 'The pharmaceutical companies do all the grafting, I see my role as nothing more than a… distributor. Fentanyl. It's fast becoming the drug of choice for the discerning smackhead.'

'Even so,' said Munro, 'let's face it, you were making a wee fortune fleecing folk who'd gone doolally. Could you not have left Carducci to get on with it, instead of slitting the poor woman's throat?'

Gundersen paused before answering.

'You surprise me with your naivety,' he said, sarcastically. 'The seedy world of pushers and users, as you call it, is worth fifty times what I made from those senile, old fools. But, it was never about the money, Munro. There was a principle at stake.'

'A principle?' said Munro, laughing as he poured himself another dram. 'Are you joking me? That takes the biscuit, I have to say. You dinnae know the meaning of the word.'

Gundersen drained his glass, placed it on the kitchen counter, and slid his hands into his pockets, his eyes glinting with a perverse delight as he sought to demolish Munro with two words.

'Do you remember a man by the name of Christy MacAdam?' he said as the more familiar deadpan expression returned to his face.

The name, yanked from the darkest recesses of his mind, hit Munro behind the eyes with the full force of a malevolent migraine.

'That mountain of blubber?' he said, grinding his teeth. 'Aye. I'll not forget him.'

'He had a head for figures. He would have made a good businessman.'

'He was a dealer!' said Munro, his lip curling with disgust. 'A good for nothing, low-life who preyed on weans who couldnae help themselves.'

'Come, come,' said Gundersen. 'He was simply exploiting a gap in the market, Munro. A very lucrative gap. It came as quite a shock to learn of his death. It was very sudden. A car park, wasn't it? Behind the Annandale Arms?'

An image of the obese MacAdam wedged firmly behind the steering wheel of his car, sweating profusely, his face riddled with fear, flashed through Munro's mind.

'Aye. It was,' he said, quietly.

'They never did find his killer, did they?' said Gundersen. 'The man who shot him in the head. Point blank. With his own gun?'

'No. I don't believe they did. Police, eh? Cannae trust them to do anything.'

Gundersen, reacting with the predictability of someone who'd undergone a humour bypass, stared blankly at Munro.

'How did it feel?' he said eventually, his voice, disarmingly soft. 'To pull that trigger?'

Munro cocked his head, wondered for a moment if he'd ever trained as a psychoanalyst, then burst into laughter as the penny dropped.

'By jiminy!' he said, as he slapped the table. 'I've got it! That's what this is all about. Christy MacAdam was working for you!'

'I lost a fortune, Munro. Overnight.'

'Well, I'm glad to hear it.'

'But you,' said Gundersen, 'I imagine, you were wallowing in glory.'

'Over an unsolved murder? No, no. That's cause for commiseration, not celebration.'

'You think you're funny, don't you?' said Gundersen. 'Did your wife think you were funny, too? A fire, wasn't it? They're easy to start. Fires. As easy as pulling a trigger. All you need is some petrol and a match. And Christy MacAdam liked to play with matches. But you know that already.'

Munro, his eyes shimmering with a sadistic rage, refused to rise to the bait.

'It must be terrible knowing that in some, small way you were responsible for her death. In fact, I feel sorry for you. Being all alone.'

Munro stared at Gundersen as a contented smile crossed his face.

'Och, I'm never alone,' he said, smugly. 'Jean is with me every second of every minute, of every hour, of every day. And that is something you'll never have. Now, I think it's time I popped my supper in the oven.'

'You don't have time to eat, Munro. I'm afraid I have an appointment to keep, so it's time for us to part company.'

'Okay, then. Cheery-bye. You can see yourself out.'

'Congratulations,' said Gundersen. 'I admire your courage. Really, I do.'

'You're too kind,' said Munro, fumbling in his coat pocket, 'but, as I've not got time to eat, I just have to send a wee text message.'

'You will do no such thing. Put your hands on the table.'

Orders, regardless of their origin – be it in the line of official duty or as a thinly-veiled threat from villains desperate to assert their authority – did not sit comfortably with Munro. Glowering across the table, he fixed Gundersen with a cold, penetrating gaze,

'See here, Gundersen,' he said, aggressively, 'I'm not bothered what happens here, do you not get that? I really couldnae give a damn. So you do, whatever it is, you have to do, but like it or not, I promised to send Charlie a text to let her know I got home safe, and you're not going to stop me. Do I make myself clear?'

Gundersen, relenting, crossed his arms and leant against the cooker as Munro continued to search his pockets.

'I cannae find the blessed phone anywhere,' he said. 'I know I had it when I left the office. Look behind you, is it on the top, by the pie?'

'No,' said Gundersen, bluntly. 'Your sad, little meal is all alone.'

Munro reached into his breast pocket and pulled out a credit card-sized piece of paper.

'Okay,' he said, 'I've the number here. You call it, then we can find it.'

'I don't have time for this Munro, I must…'

'Call the damn number! Do you hear me?'

Gundersen, taken aback, reluctantly pulled the phone from his pocket.

'Very well,' he said, angrily. 'Hurry up.'

'Okay. 07532 442 292,' said Munro as the card slipped from his fingers.

'292,' said Gundersen, holding his phone aloft. 'I hope for your sake you hear it ring.'

'If I do,' said Munro, as he bent to retrieve the card from the floor, 'it'll be a catastrophe. Aye, that's the word. A catastrophe.'

Epilogue

For the residents of the village – where the rustle of a crisp packet was deemed a major disturbance and the highlight of the social calendar was electing a new chair to the parish council – the unprecedented sight of grey plumes of smoke drifting against a clear, moonlit sky, as the blue lights of the fire engines bounced off the whitewashed cottages was, despite the acrid stench of burning timbers, a spectacle to behold.

West, flanked by Dougal to her left and Duncan on her right, blamed the caustic fumes for her watery eyes as they ducked under the tape, marched along the narrow road and stood staring silently at what was left of Munro's house.

'It's not as bad as I thought,' said Dougal. 'Most of it's still standing.'

'Most of the damage is round is the back,' said Duncan. 'Well, that's what they said on the phone, anyway. Miss? Are you okay?'

West turned and smiled.

'Yeah, fine,' she said, desperately trying not to fall apart. 'We should take a look.'

'You don't have to do this,' said Duncan, 'you know that, don't you? As the chief says, take-offs are optional, but landings are mandatory. You'll not be able to unsee anything in there.'

'Hold on,' said Dougal, 'white-top's coming out.'

The fire chief, his face glistening with sweat, walked towards them, visibly annoyed that, despite the tape, some members of the public felt it their God-given right to ignore safety procedures to get a closer look.

'You lot,' he said, raising his hands, 'that cordon's there for a reason. Now take yourselves back down the street before I…'

West held up her warrant card.

'… call the police. That's handy. Are you the investigating officer?'

'No,' said West. 'We're colleagues of the bloke who lives here. He's a police officer.'

'Sorry to hear that, but you still can't go inside, not until we've given the all clear.'

'What happened?' said Duncan. 'There was talk of a loud bang.'

The fire chief removed his helmet and wiped his forehead with the back of his sleeve.

'That's an understatement,' he said with a sigh. 'Gas explosion.'

'That bloody cooker!' said West, stamping the ground. 'I knew it was a death trap. It was like something out the dark ages.'

'No, no,' said the chief, reassuringly. 'It's not the cooker, it was perfectly sound.'

'So, what are you saying? That this was some kind of freak accident?'

'Look, we'll have to wait until the Fire Investigation Unit have done a full survey to be sure, okay? But if it was an accident, then yes. It was very freaky, indeed.'

'Come again?' said West.

'The gas for the oven was turned up full, and probably had been for quite some time. Thing is, it hadn't been lit.'

'So, there was a massive build-up of gas?' said Dougal. 'Is that it?'

'Aye. Exactly.'

'Well, he could've just forgotten,' said West. 'I mean, he's been pretty stressed out lately, we all have. He could've turned it on and walked away to…'

'No, no,' said the chief. 'See, we also found a mobile phone…'

'Well, that's not…'

'In the oven.'

West stared at the chief, her eyes wide with disbelief.

'I don't get it,' she said, shaken, 'I mean, why would he…?'

'Here's the thing. Gas and electricity, see, they're not the best of friends, so, too much gas, call the number, an arc occurs, and boom. If it was deliberate, and I'm not qualified to say for sure, then hats off to the fella. Very ingenious, indeed.'

'If it was deliberate?' said Dougal. 'But why on earth would he stick his phone in the oven?'

The chief, his face black with soot, regarded West with sympathetic eyes.

'You said he was stressed out,' he said. 'Could he have been depressed about anything?'

'Oh, no, no,' said West, laughing nervously as he she held up her hands. 'Don't even go there. Suicide? Jimbo? No, forget it.'

'What about the phone?' said Duncan. 'Has that been blown to smithereens?'

'No, no,' said the chief. 'See, because this wasn't a mains leak, it was contained, to an extent. Let me explain – in a situation like this, when the gas pops, like anything else, it looks for the path of least resistance – the door. So, it was like firing a canon. The blaze that follows is very intense but only for a very short period of time, it's like flash-frying a steak. So, regarding the phone, there's some damage, of course, and I can't guarantee it hasn't cooked the components, but there's a chance you might get something off it. You might even find out who called the number.'

'You have no idea how helpful that is,' said Dougal. 'Thanks.'

* * *

Fearful that her next question may see her crumble like a sandcastle in the incoming tide, West, as stoical as ever, regarded the chief in a manner befitting a patient in oncology awaiting the results of an MRI scan.

'So,' she said, nibbling at her fingernails, 'have you... I mean... did you find anyone?'

'Aye, he's bagged up on the front lawn.'

'Bagged up on the lawn?' said Duncan, scowling. 'Jesus, man, have you no respect? You make him sound like an oven-ready turkey!'

'It's okay,' said West, allowing herself a smile, 'it's just the kind of thing Jimbo would've said.'

* * *

Standing over the body bag, Dougal, unable to contain his excitement, grinned at West as though he'd been nominated to open a surprise present, as she, Duncan, and the fire chief gathered round.

'That stupid grin had better be a part of your coping mechanism, or so help me God...'

'It's not him!' said Dougal, beaming. 'Look at the size of him, it's too tall.'

'Don't be so bloody ridiculous, for God's sake, Dougal, if you don't...'

'Hey, hey, come on now,' said Duncan, 'that's no way to behave, is it? Do you think he'd have wanted to see you two acting like a pair of kids?'

'Sorry, you're right,' said West, contritely. 'Come on then. Let's get this over with.'

'Hold on,' said the fire chief, as he knelt by the top of the bag, 'I should warn you, it's not a pleasant sight. He's suffered flash burns to his face and hands, his hair's all but gone, and his clothes, well, they're more like a second skin now.'

'Crap,' said West, having second thoughts as she tucked her arm round Dougal's.

'Did he… I mean, would he have felt anything?'

'On the plus side, no,' said the chief. 'Look, I know it's not much, but if it's any consolation, he didn't feel a thing. It was the force of the blast that killed him. Blew the oven door clean off its hinges and took him with it. It was instant.'

'Well, that's something I suppose.'

'There is one other thing,' said the chief. 'You'll find out sooner or later, so…'

'Oh God,' said West, 'go on. What is it?'

'I reckon he was standing right by the cooker when it blew. I'm afraid anything below the waist is pretty much in tatters.'

West spun on her feet, pulled a handkerchief from her pocket and wiped her eyes.

'Okay,' she said, taking a deep breath as she turned around. 'Open it.'

The chief unzipped the bag to the shoulders and paused before pulling it apart.

'That's me off crispy duck for the foreseeable,' said Duncan as Dougal burst into fits of hysterical laughter.

'Gundersen!' he said. 'What did I tell you? I knew it! Did I not say…?'

'Yes, you did,' said West, bluntly.

'I knew I should've stayed,' said Duncan, growling under his breath. 'I said to him, I said, chief, will I come inside and he said no. He said he'd be fine.'

'He would, wouldn't he?' said West, reeling from the shock that the char-grilled cadaver wasn't Munro.

'Gundersen,' said Duncan, morosely. 'He must've waited until I left before...'

'I don't get it,' said Dougal, befuddled. 'What's going on here? That's not the DI lying there, that's Gundersen in the bag. Is that not good news?'

West, stared blankly at Dougal, her eyes misting over.

'No,' she said, softly. 'It's not good at all.'

'Why?'

'Because, you numpty,' said Duncan, angrily, 'if Gundersen's out here, that means...'

'Oh, Christ!' said Dougal. 'Sorry. I wasn't thinking.'

'There's no telling what this murderous bastard's done to him.'

West, her heart pounding, waited until the fire chief had zipped up the bag before broaching the inevitable.

'Okay,' she said, clearing her throat, 'let's get this over with.'

'Sorry, Sergeant, you've lost me,' said the chief, donning his helmet.

'The other body. Where is it? Inside?'

'There is no other body. That's it. Just the one fatality.'

'No, that can't be right,' said Duncan. 'I left the chief at home probably not more than twenty minutes before this happened.'

'I'm telling you, there's no-one else.'

'And you're sure?' said West. 'Beyond a shadow of a doubt?'

'Absolutely, one hundred per cent,' said the chief. 'Look, I know this is upsetting, and I hate to disappoint you, but we've combed every inch of that house from top to bottom and I can assure you, there's definitely no-one else inside.'

West, succumbing to shock, turned to Dougal as her eyes glazed over.

'Where the hell is he?' she said, her voice trembling. 'Where the bloody hell has he gone?'

Character List

DI JAMES MUNRO – Shrewd, smart and cynical with an inability to embrace retirement, Munro has to deal with a figure from his distant past intent on bringing him down, once and for all.

DS CHARLOTTE WEST – Finally overcoming her self-doubt, "Charlie" takes the reigns as the investigating officer when an old adversary turns up like a bad penny. Fortunately for her, she has DI Munro, father-figure and mentor, to steer her in the right direction.

DC DOUGAL McCRAE – A clever, young and unintentionally single introvert with more brains than brawn who'd rather be fishing than drinking in the pub.

DC DUNCAN REID – Wet behind the ears as a DC but laid-back and brimming with confidence, his mission is to seek out the seedy side of life and destroy it.

DCI GEORGE ELLIOT – Laid back and relaxed, happy behind a desk and happiest at home, he prefers to let others do the dirty work having spent a lifetime dicing with death.

FATHER CALLUM DALGETTY – An ageing priest whose faith begins to wane after the unexpected loss of his lifelong friend and soul mate.

ALISON KENNEDY – Manager of the Glencree care home, she's kind, smart, and foxy and knows a thing or two about playing the field.

LUCAS RIETVELD – Tall, dark, and Dutch, a solicitor, and a ladies' man with the ability to drain their bank accounts at the drop of a hat.

LARS GUNDERSEN – A Norwegian with a split personality who'll stop at nothing to satisfy his lust for wealth and bring down his nemesis.

JASMINDER BANERJEE – Married to Aletta, "Jazz" is the proud owner of Kestrel Cars, works like a dog and is on the lookout for ways to supplement his income.

ANITA CARDUCCI – Widow to Remo, she's fresh out of jail and keen to pick up where she left off, until a complication thwarts her plans.

CLARE MacALLISTER – Avoiding a jail term by the skin of her teeth, she's moving in the wrong circles and soon finds herself without an alibi.

If you enjoyed this book, please let others know by leaving a quick review on Amazon. Also, if you spot anything untoward in the paperback, get in touch. We strive for the best quality and appreciate reader feedback.

editor@thebookfolks.com

www.thebookfolks.com

ALSO BY PETE BRASSETT

In this series:

SHE – book 1
AVARICE – book 2
ENMITY – book 3
DUPLICITY – book 4
TALION – book 6
PERDITION – book 7
RANCOUR – book 8
PENITENT – book 9

Other titles:

THE WILDER SIDE OF CHAOS
YELLOW MAN
CLAM CHOWDER AT LAFAYETTE AND SPRING
THE GIRL FROM KILKENNY
BROWN BREAD
PRAYER FOR THE DYING
KISS THE GIRLS

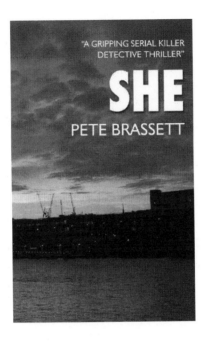

SHE

With a serial killer on their hands, Scottish detective
Munro and rookie sergeant West must act fast to trace a
woman placed at the scene of crime. Yet discovering her
true identity, let alone finding her, proves difficult. Soon
they realise the crime is far graver than either of them
could have imagined.

AVARICE

A sleepy Scottish town, a murder in a glen. The local
police chief doesn't want a fuss and calls in DI Munro to
lead the investigation. But Munro is a stickler for
procedure, and his sidekick Charlie West has a nose for a
cover up. Someone in the town is guilty, will they find out
who?

ENMITY

When it comes to frustrating a criminal investigation, this
killer has all the moves. A spate of murders is causing
havoc among in a remote Scottish town. Enter Detective
Inspector Munro to catch the red herrings and uncover an
elaborate and wicked ruse.

DUPLICITY

When a foreign worker casually admits to the murder of a
local businessman, detectives in a small Scottish town
guess that the victim's violent death points to a more
complex cause. Money appears to be a motive, but will
anyone believe that they might be in fact dealing with a
crime of passion?

TALION

A boy finds a man's body on a beach. Police quickly suspect foul play when they discover he was part of a local drugs ring. With no shortage of suspects, they have a job pinning anyone down. But when links to a local business are discovered, it seems the detectives may have stumbled upon a much bigger crime than they could have imagined.

PERDITION

A man is found dead in his car. A goat is killed with a crossbow. What connects these events in a rural Scottish backwater? DI Charlotte West investigates in this gripping murder mystery that ends with a sucker punch of a twist.

RANCOUR

When the body of a girl found on a mountainside tests positive for a date rape drug, police suspect a local Lothario is responsible. He certainly had the means, motive and opportunity. But is this really such a cut and dry case? What are the detectives missing?

PENITENT

A missing pensioner. A boxer who keeps getting beat. A woman found dead in the municipal pool. DI Charlie West is charged with finding the connection between these events. As she investigates, the shady past of a small town and a legacy of regret and resentment surfaces.

For more great books, visit: www.thebookfolks.com